The Reaper's Blood

Book 1 of The Bloo̦

THE REAPER'S BLOODHOUND

GRACE OKOT

To a future I never thought I could reach.

TAGGED

She's known as the Mother of Wolves.

Scarlet tears stream down my chin as Oliver's words pierce through my brain.

If you end up in her domain, you better pray she ends you swiftly.

Threaded lines carve into my face as agonizing cries rip at my throat. *It was such a vague warning... Oliver! That damn witch*! My whiskers scrape against the metal as the muzzle clamps my jaw shut. Leather straps slap against my head, begetting a stream of mucus pouring down my black nose as Oliver's voice continues to resound in my ears.

Because as pleasant as her lair may look, she's not known as the guardian of ravenous, wild beasts for nothing.

She was right. Flames blaze against my cheeks, and gashes scatter across my coat as puss excretes from the blisters shrouding my body. Thick bands from the muzzle's belt gnaws at my flesh, and my claws drill into the scratched tiles as raspy breaths erupt from my throat. *It hurts. It hurts so damn much.* The rubber bands tighten against my face, and my bloodshot eyes wince as the shadow of a round figure penetrates my view.

I wiggle myself away from its dark gaze, but the more I cower, the more the metallic gleams pierce my stinging eyes and cause my sliced face to scrunch in confusion.

Silhouettes sway in my view, rattling against one another as their faint forms gradually become clearer. Choke collars, break sticks, shock leashes, and equipment able to take down a werewolf, dangle upon the blood-stained walls thirsting for their next victim. My chipped ears flatten against my head as a whimper protrudes from my lips. Like an empty dam once filled with endless tears, my eyes crystallize, and my lungs ache as I force myself to cry.

"Please…" I mumble, staring hazily at the shadows lurking at the back of the room, "help me."

But I know, no matter how much my glossy eyes and trembling lips plead, the werewolves I've once called 'brother' are a fathomless abyss that only sink my calls into a bottomless pit of despair.

"Help? It's your fault."

Goosebumps crawl against my skin as the devil's voice brushes against my ears. Her smoky breath digs into my nostrils, and her icy hand lands upon my temple as her frill dress collar runs along my pale face. Hot mucus bubbles from my nose, and my paws hurriedly scrape at the silver slabs as my chains clatter against the concrete.

Every inch of my body is screaming at me to leave, to escape this place. Thorns prod at my chest, with foam oozing from my black lips as I scamper to the back of the boxed room. Vans boom behind an iron door dwelling amidst the gloom, and the spikes piercing my lungs gradually dissolve into straws nesting against my ribcage. *I can do it. I can get out!*

My thick palm draws towards the comfort of the bustling road, stretching as if freedom is within a hand's reach. The night's light from the barred windows seeps through my webbed feet, caressing my torn face and edging me nearer, but my breath hitches, and not because of the satisfaction of my release.

Brambles crush my heart, and red clouds my vision. A screech jerks my body as my brain hits against my skull, and my body slams into the tiled floor.

"I wouldn't do that if I were you," Dean whispers, coiling her tanned hands around my neck, as she clips a black collar against my skin.

Her apple-red lips lift into a snarky smile as I struggle to swallow the thick blood plugging my throat.

"It suits you," she says lowly, combing through my damp fur. "Think of it as a reminder of our little secret." Dean's cigarette tears at my bodysuit, and the sizzle of my flesh bounces off the ashen walls as a high-pitched scream leaves my mouth, "That you'll keep, won't you?"

Salty droplets line my eyes as the burning scent of my skin presses against the roof of my mouth. My throbbing wounds cry out, and the chains wounding my body aren't helping in the slightest, as it coils around my limbs and coats its steel in an ominous red.

"N-no…" I mutter, my fangs glistening at her crimson-haired frame.

"Oh?" Dean's smile drops, and her brows lift as her face contorts in confusion. "But don't you need this job?"

Cracks infiltrate my ears as my head crashes against the concrete.

"For yourself?"

Stings zap my body as the muzzle weighs deeper into my skin.

"For your family, perhaps?"

Blood pours down my nose as a growl erupts from my chest, and the tension in Dean's hand slightly loosens around my neck.

"I can't find a reason for you to say no," she says childishly, "You passed on my property. Don't you think you should be considering yourself lucky to even have your life spared, intruder?"

Dean's slanted eyes penetrate my skull, and my stomach turns. The haunting clink of metal weapons, swinging from the sharp-edged, wooden, frame board, at my back, loops in my rounded ears like a ticking time bomb. Night light trickles onto the opaque glass behind Dean, and its pale glow brings an illuminated show as it highlights my suffering to those feeling a sense of amusement on the other side. *To think I expected kindness, pity, help.* My nails dig into the arms holding me as I hesitantly meet Dean's burning gaze. *The thought itself is taboo.*

"What…Job…" I murmur.

Murky yellow teeth, dark in contrast to the flames of red hair sitting upon Dean's scalp, beam at me as I writhe within her grasp.

"Are we getting to an understanding?" she questions, pressing her nails into my skin. "Then be my Watchdog. Warn them, hurt them, kill them, I don't care what methods you choose. Just don't let me see a single one of your 'kin' making the same mistake you did, alright?"

My body drops to the floor as Dean's grip releases, and she fixes the oversized sunglasses atop her head.

"It's either that, or you become a Stray," she states, "and guaranteeing your life on that one is quite slim. We don't want that now, do we?"

She gestures to a purple liquid in the hands of a werewolf guarding the exit as she sneers at me. "Your answer?"

The taste of iron accumulates upon my tongue as my cuts begin to swell. Chains gnaw at my wrists, weighing me to the floor and limiting my movement. Blood slides down my raven fur, masking the burning, bald patches received from Deianira D. Lobos' equipment. *Yet, I promised.* A hiss escapes my lips as I clutch my beaten body. *I promised him 'I wasn't going to break Pack Code!'* My feet tremble from the pain surging through me, and my jaw clamps as I inhale the iron scent seeping from the muzzle. *A slight mistake won't stop me from keeping my word.* My yellow eyes glare at the Beast Tamer's pompous physique, the notorious figure known as the 'Mother of Wolves', and a snarl reaches my lips. *Even if it's you, Deianira.*

"I'll do it."

Dean's wrinkles refine as her face beams. Her arms stick out to what seems to be an empty embrace, as she stoops to my quivering figure. "Then it looks like we'll get along, Gabriel."

THE RETIRED BEAST

My eyes fling open as strangled cries emerge from my throat. Gasps of air plummet down my airways, and my trembling fingers dig into my scarlet chest as goosebumps pop against my wet skin. Tears slither down my cheeks as raspy breaths protrude from my mouth, and the wrinkles of my damp shirt loosens as my strained knuckles release its grip. *Calm down.* My needled hairs gradually flatten as my palm rubs against my swollen eyes. *It's been two weeks; I'm safe.*

My eyes narrow as the sun's rays beam against my face and filter through the semi-transparent curtains, touching upon my digital clock's black sheen. Its glaring glimmer illuminates the small room, and its blue digits shift once the minutes pass. *'8:47'.* My eyes hazily stare at the plaid mattress, clasped by steel bars, as it hangs atop the top bunk's frame. *It's no surprise I can't hear a thing.*

I groan as I make my way to the bathroom with a cold sweat trailing down my body. Bile clambers up my throat, and my stomach churns as my legs ache to buckle. It's like a mile, every step sapping my strength as I press myself against the oak door. It isn't long before globs of red slush blind my view, and my energy depletes once the stench of stale meat crawls into my nostrils. *Damn it.* My head droops onto the toilet bowl as my hand rubs against my bitter lips. *It happened again.*

The tap creaks as I brace the cold water splattering onto my burnt umber hands. The icy fluid seeps into my arm sleeves and closes my pores as it drips against my skin.

What have I done? The same question appears in my head the more I wake up from that nightmare. Along with the scar stretching across my jaw - haunting me from that night. My wet palms slide along the self-inflicted wound marked against my chest. *Was it the right thing?* But when those star-filled, brown eyes look at me from that torn, rectangular frame atop the silver porcelain, the time to regret my actions is non-existent – for everything I've done, it's only been for Daniel. My hands lift as the graze fades, revealing a smooth, dark sheet of cedar brown beneath the inked fabric. I reach up to the black collar latched upon my neck and clasp it tightly within my bony hands.

Transmissions regarding 'work' buzz like a set of flies, and never ceases to blare as I spam the mute icon repeatedly. Countless beeps emanate from the collar as I head out of the dorm, and its elevated cries only add a second verse to the static interference projecting from the speaker. *Great.*

Shouts and roars emerge from the T.V room as I step out, and my head begins to pound. Behind a large, glass window, werewolves cluster around wide-screen boxes of the wealthy crowd that owned them hollering within Lacuna Dome. Mimicking the actions of the rich, the werewolves jump in place to the action presented at the arena, as the victor of the present match becomes apparent.

"Once again, ladies and gentlemen," The commentator screams, spitting into his mic, "Jay Vigolfr, our ruthless fighter, is the winner of today's Wolf Fight!"

Cheers echo within the Dome as the commentator points to a savage brute whose brown, sunken eyes dye black and teeth ruthlessly dig into his opponent's chest. Blood splatters onto his sun-wash undercoat, and his blood-stained fangs glisten in the refracted light as they emerge from his ripped lips like a sly grin.

His head propels once again, lunging for another bite, but a choke collar pulls his neck, and the sharp cracks of countless sticks echo in the arena as Gladiators struggle to hold him down. A thunderous roar shakes the stadium and the beast, with black spikes jutting from his body, tackles anybody who dares to approach. Though, the human's alloy isn't easy to resist, and handcuffs that pinch the skin grip onto his wrists as electric shocks strike his system once a steel muzzle clips onto his head. Sneers plaster onto the Gladiators' faces, and they revel in the crowd's booming cheers as the submission of the spitting, immobilized beast appears before them. Even if the winner of today's contest is the thrashing barbarian, the glory goes to the 'Guardians' - taking control of a 'wild animal's uncontrollable persistence' - the Gladiators.

"Hard to take down!" The commentator yells as the television booms with the intensity of his voice, "As expected of Kirkos' runner-up for Top Dog! But are guts simply all it takes?"

The enthralled crowd of Beast Tamers screams at the top of their lungs, and the claw marks on my wrists begin to ache despite being inflicted ages ago. Werewolves peer at the screen in awe, as the results of today's match adorn the walls of the boxed room on sheets of white paper drawn in red marker. Motivation bubbles within their systems as their eyes glisten with envy, want, the desire for strength, but is becoming Top Dog really worth it?

I shrink towards the Cafeteria's exit and embrace the wind caressing my dark, chocolate skin. My white shirt flutters in the cool breeze as pebbles crackle beneath my beige sandals, and the whiff of wolfsbane intoxicates me, slapping me in the face, thrusting needles into my chest, and making my head's throbbing even worse as it slides down my throat. Yet, something about it makes me relax, makes me seem human, and makes me forget about the blood-thirsty monster lurking within me; *the werewolf that I am.*

I stop to stare at the round-petalled flowers swaying nonchalantly in the breeze. Their powerful scent oozes from their stems as Caretakers harvest them for the upcoming festival, Lupercalia. Rays of light bask onto their glowing bodies as they pluck at the purple orchids with gloved hands, too weak to harm a Werewolf, but if holding a weapon - could kill if given the chance.

A sneeze shoots from my mouth as I trudge up the weed-blanketed staircase and come face-to-face with the ancient, wooden, wolf shrine, the humans used to worship, sitting in the middle of an empty field. The holy temple of my brethren totters as I walk past it, but unlike me, it remains tall and firm, as it refuses to be knocked down by a light breeze.

I press my back into the long blades of grass, relishing in the quiet atmosphere, and I take a deep breath. The air is cleaner here, the scent of the purple flower seemingly faint and less toxic. Other werewolves will have to venture the sea of wolfsbane to come here, so the unlikeliness of meeting one is extremely delightful.

Gusts of wind pull at my curls as lines of the walls, caging werewolves within their sector, emerges in the distance. Slim trees at the edge of the circular plain bend as their fallen leaves brush against my cool cheeks. And for a second, I'm wishing time could just stand still.

"Gabriel Louvell?"

My head whips to meet the eyes of a small, raven-haired girl, peering behind the temple in layers of baggy clothing.

"Who-"

"It is." A sigh of relief escapes her mouth as soft tones slide from her tongue, "I thought…I'd find you here."

"So, you stalked me?"

Hairs rise at the back of my neck as a growl erupts from my chest. *A sane wolf will never come to such a poisonous place. Yet you found me? By coincidence, at that.*

"N-no!" she cries, fiddling with her fingers as if to take back the sudden rise of her voice. Her head drops to the ground as her words fade into a whisper. "I found you, you were there, and I thought I could just ask to make sure, and-"

"Well, what do you want?"

Tears well within the girl's eyes as she flinches at my rough tone. Her head bows deeper into her collar as she plays with the hem of her cable-knit poncho.

"A-advice," she squeaks.

"And you think I'd just give it to you?"

The girl peeks at me like a frightened hare about to succumb to the fangs of a wolf, and her lips tremble as she speaks.

"It's just..." her eyes flicker towards me, then to the ground as she gulps, "I've been a fan of yours for a long time… and I just thought…"

I grit my teeth as I pull my arm sleeves. *Does she remember?* The scars on my wrists and legs are more of an eyesore than the desired trophy. Yet, some werewolves remembered? My eyes narrow as my legs itch to flee with the silhouette of the girl's figure ingrained into my pupils. Though if I evade, I'm simply a weakling clothed in the façade of a wolf; a failure.

"Fine, keep it short," I grunt, as her face beams with sparkling eyes and a smile that lights her happiness even further.

The girl meddles with her turtle-neck collar, and picks at the small holes with her short beige fingertips till her grin fades. She shuffles beside me without a word and sends me quick glances as she pushes her feet deeply into the ground. Only the rushing water of the pond and gentle winds surround us, as the two of us remain a distance of a few metres, the same width of the temple behind us.

My eyes run over her fidgeting figure. She isn't saying a word. Silence passes through us like waves as the anticipation of what she has to say and the wasting of my time penetrates my brain.

I impatiently turn to the girl's frame, and my lips curl upwards, "Hey-"

"I...I have my first fight today," she starts, clenching and unclenching her hands as if they're working up a sweat. She exhales deeply before hiding her hands behind the centre of her back. "But I'm facing someone who's so much bigger, faster, stronger... everything I'm not."

The young girl shivers with glossy eyes begging to pour droplets onto her red cheeks as she turns away.

"Sorry," she whimpers, rubbing her crimson eyes with the sleeves of her oat jumper, "I knew I'd be this hopeless when I first arrived, but now that I have to fight...I-"

Her sobs sound in my ears as I pick at the stalks of grass. Like a low murmur, her sniffles quieten as they disperse within the soft breeze, and as she composes herself, my lips begin to move on their own. "Coming here was your first mistake."

The girl's amber hues widen as they turn to meet my steel, grey ones.

"From what I see, you're probably more suited to raise pups in the community and look after the elders," I state, as the girl bites her lip and narrows her eyes, shaking her head in disagreement.

"I can't," she mutters, "I can't."

"Then you should take a look at reality if you expect to progress in this line of work without risking anything," I say, sucking my teeth under my breath as I turn my head away from her. *Who does she think she is? Human?* A scoff leaves my throat. *Werewolves live to fight. Do you think we'd be here if the world gave us anything for free!?*

"But I can't just stay and do nothing while my brother's fighting for his life either!" she cries as a tear runs down her buttoned nose.

A sigh escapes my lips as her body trembles, "But does your brother feel the same?"

Her lips part slightly, but the words formulating upon her tongue lie jumbled. "He-…I'm sorry…"

Her eyes bear a reddish hue from the tears she's holding back, and blood pours down her lip. "It was selfish of me to think you could help me…"

My heart pangs against my chest. Her small physique as she turns, weak and fragile, I've seen it before. Daniel, a snotty, weak, and selfish brat, who can break with the slightest push yet never listens, has the same figure.

My hand stretches out to grab her startled frame, crying a waterfall of tears from her small, monolid eyes as her canine pierces her lips.

"I know it's none of my business," I say, wiping the blood dripping from her chin. "But I still think you should consider what I've said."

My large, cold hands lightly press onto the wound as she flinches against my touch. *The bite mark isn't closing.* Even though it's such a small wound, it refuses to close. *What slow regeneration.*

"It might've been a bit harsh, especially to a fan of mine, but I'll be hearing my bad deed to no end if I let you go," I say, tightening my hold on her thin wrist. "So, forgive me this one time?"

The girl fights against my grip, flailing her arms as my hold on her only tightens. "I-I don't think-"

"When I first fought, I thought, 'if your opponent's bigger than you, take advantage of your leg length." My grip loosens as her glassy eyes no longer flow with endless tears, "Kick your opponent here," I advise, gesturing to my knee, "and maintain your distance. If it works out, it will-'"

A striking pain escalates my leg as I drop to the floor. Pins and needles tingle in my limb, as the girl gapes at my squirming form as if she's witnessing a miracle.

"Are you serious!?" I hiss, massaging the footprint imprinted on my knee joint.

"It worked…"

"You don't say," I state, rolling my eyes and sighing as I did so. "But I couldn't grab you, right?"

"Y-yeah," she stutters, wiggling with excitement.

"The enemy is at their weakest when fazed." My palm rubs against my face, and my eyes narrow, tracing the scar that will follow me into the grave. "If you wanted, you could've gone for my neck," I say, forcing a laugh.

The girl digs her thumb's nail into her fingers. "Will I-"

I gaze at her bare neck as she squirms beside me; she doesn't have a collar. How many days has it been since I've spoken to someone from Bronze Rank? The constant fighting, just to show your worth, just to appeal to the audience. At times, I wonder how I'd lived through such an anxious phase.

I put a hand to her back. "You're going into a trial battle. Gladiators keep a close eye on the matches."

Large eyes glisten at me like a dog anticipating a treat, and my brows furrow.

"It's a safe place." I lie.

The girl's head perks as if she could hear the slight doubt in my voice, and my gaze fixates upon the short blades of grass. *How can I assure you if I can't even convince myself?* Static filters through my radio collar, and my eyes run over the silver box attached to it, as an 'important' announcement cancels the awkward silence between us.

"Then uhm…thank you," she says with a light smile creasing her sandy cheeks, "And I'm sorry… for troubling you…and everything…I'll go before my match starts."

"But uh… your name?"

The girl gawks at me as if I'm speaking a foreign language. She opens, then shuts her mouth, her jaw clamping as she scratches her neatly lined brows.

"M-Maya," she mumbles with a blush creeping onto her cream skin.

"Then, Good luck, Maya," I say, returning her smile.

"Thank you."

As smooth as a new-born pup, Maya's face beams with delight from those two words, and she vanishes below the concrete staircase like mist dispersing on an early afternoon. The smile she upheld erases from her face as she turns, and the sweet, warm, milky scent she gives off is soon replaced with the purple flowers' pungent odours stinging my nose.

"What do you want?" I groan, turning on my radio collar's transmission.

"You cold-hearted son-of-a-bitch! What do you mean, 'what do you want'?"

My hand slams against the speaker as Nathan's yelling punctures my ears.

"I've been contacting you for over an hour!" he yells, as the high altitude of his volume causes me to wince.

"Sorry to break it to you, but your voice isn't great on the ears, Nathan."

Nathan grunts as his voice teems with impatience, "It's just you. The ladies love me for it."

I scoff, "I can assure you're being lied to."

"You-" A sigh escapes Nathan's lips as his face twitching in annoyance is visible in my mind. "This is why you have no friends besides me, man."

A snort escapes my mouth as a murmur of various voices emerges within the background. Nathan's shuffling emits from the speaker as he moves to a more discrete place, "I'll let that slide just this once. This is urgent."

My brows furrow. *I don't want to hear it – he'll only contact me for one reason.* Nathan lowers his voice till his breath prickles against my skin. As the words fall from his tongue, the colour from my face doesn't take long to follow after. His gruff tone infiltrates my ears, and the more I analyse every letter, the more I regret picking up this call.

"Dean's called for you. You have your first assignment."

TARGET

he Witch's lips lift into a snarky smile as the hairs at the back of my neck rise. Murky claws protrude from my fingernails as my pearly whites jut out of my jaw, glistening in the room's ambient light whilst awaiting the tear of the witch's pale flesh. An irritable grin plasters onto her face, and she waves her middle finger brazenly into the air while whistling as if she's calling a dog. *Bitch.* I lunge at her with fangs anxious for the kill, ready to rip her apart, careless of the animal decorations littered in Dean's room, and my head lurches forward with a chuckle emitting from the witch's devilish lips. A folder slides down my leg, and a smirk stretches across Nathan's face as my hand rubs against my scalp.

"It's about time," Nathan stresses, picking up the file and shoving it against my chest.

My transformation regresses as I glower at his happy-go-lucky demeanour circling around me without an utter of an apology.

"Leave him," Dean says, slouching at her desk with a sneer plastering onto her oily face. Her diamond, square rings dig into her neck as she clasps her large hands underneath her round chin, "our newbie's just having trouble adjusting."

I grunt as my head turns to Oliver's dark blue irises, threatening me from across the room: *"Make a scene. I dare you."* Like a raging storm over turbulent seas, plunging me to the ocean floor, her ruinous eyes confine and crush me as effortlessly as an ant. Her snarky smile pierces through me like a bullet from the guns hanging beneath the glass cabinets, and a shiver shoots down my spine. *Don't think you'll be smiling for much longer.* I snarl as I concentrate on the file in front of me.

Different backgrounds and descriptions of werewolves within the facility lie scribbled upon the pages - their rank, names, age, siblings, birthdate, blood type, etc.

My fingers loiter on a square picture encircled in red marker. A boy with dark, sunken, monolid eyes glares at me from the pages. Fierce, dark-swept brows mark his face, contrasting the short, black, voluminous, bowl cut covering his head. Sparse lashes adorn his round, baby face, and the name *'Jay Vigolfr'* reads beside the image which makes my heart sink.

"Blood Type, A?" I mutter, the words barely evident as they fall off my tongue.

"It's not often you find a gem as rare as that," Dean coos, with an alluring voice that makes me stiffen, "but it just so happens, I'm not the only one looking out for him, you see."

Dean sighs as she strides towards me. Her thick-heeled, black boots clack against the mahogany tiles as she winds her arms around my shoulders. Her white, fur coat scratches against my cheeks, and I tense under her touch as she presses her thin, red lips against my ear.

"So do me a favour, Gabriel." she says, with the scent of tobacco overpowering my sense of smell. "Let's protect him. Together."

Together? You and me? Dean's face lights up as my dusky, yellow eyes pierce through her smirking figure. *What bullshit.*

"You're planning to buy him!" I snap, gritting my teeth to hold back the fury seething inside of me.

Dean puts her hands up in defence as she releases her hold on my shoulders, "Oh no, no, no. I plan to get the majority of what goes around." she corrects, silencing me with her sea-weed green eyes. "Do you think there's something wrong with that?"

The document crumples in my grasp, and my claws thirst to soak in her blood. My nails pierce into my palms, filling my nails with dead skin as I take a deep breath. "No, ma'am." I close my eyelids as the file shuts in my trembling hands.

Dean chuckles lowly, and passes her orange hands through the dark coils fixed against my scalp as her eyes trace my figure. "Then I'm looking forward to a good job, or you'll be kissing that contract of ours goodbye. But I'm sure you wouldn't do that, would you?"

My eyes narrow as I bite my lip. Dean's gaze lingers on me as my head sinks and sights drop to the tiger rug sprawled across the wooden floor. My hands ball into a fist as I shake my head hesitantly.

Dean's thick hand slides along the back of my neck, and a smug grin embellishes her oiled face, "As expected of my employee. You're dismissed."

My tall frame exits the room as a snicker leaves Oliver's mouth. Nathan runs to my side, slinging his hand across my shoulder, quick enough to block my curling lips and furrowing brows at the she-wolf's skeletal figure.

He nudges me onward, and we pass through the gateway leading to the Werewolves' quarters. Large slabs of stone hang over our heads as an icy current, I'm too late to brace myself from, slams onto our bare bodies.

Kirkos' Gate; the unreasonably big passageway looms over us as we take our leave. Camouflaging into the clouds on a grey day, and ten times the height and width of the Beast Tamer's lorries occasionally going in and out, gusts of wind lash at us from the excess amount of empty space claiming to be the 'entrance' of the gate. If anything, it could've been a gateway to heaven, a werewolf's Utopia, but the reality is far from that.

The gazes of Gladiators stab our backs like a set of knives as we walk past. Red uniforms and weapons fill our view as the 'Guardians' don't take a single eye off of our bodies, as if simply breathing is a sin. My hand grips onto my radio collar. *I'd do anything to throw it – destroy it.* Yet my dead body struck by silver bullets and countless aluminium arrows will be the last thing I'd see, if this black collar of identification didn't remain strapped in this restricted zone.

A stifled grunt escapes my throat as an arch welcomes our presence whilst towering over our heads. White light bounces from the marble tiles' surface, and gleams at us once we step into the lobby. Half walls adorn the lobby's corners with potted plants sitting upon their surfaces, as they stretch their growing limbs into the surrounding communal areas on opposite sides. Every compartment is the same size, with the same chalky walls, the same, red-inked posters, and the same mirrored tiles flashing their blinding lights into your eyes - a place no different from a pup's toy house. A maze.

"Looks like she has her favourites," I grumble, swatting Nathan's brawny arm as we stop at my locker, deeply situated within the lobby. The rusty piece of garbage groans as it protests, and I reluctantly take out one of the many syringes lined at the door with a scowl on my face.

"You're new, trust takes time," Nathan says, re-adjusting his giant hands on my head instead. "Plus, your attitude is crap; who wouldn't suspect you?"

I sigh as the imprint of Dean's hand still lingers on my scalp as Nathan messes up my black curls. The bleach-scented syringe sinks into my skin, filling with a mouthful of my blood as I tug at the facility's bodysuit. Such a powerful chemical cloaking this metal syringe due to being re-used by many other werewolves - *It makes me sick.*

"Seriously, if you toned down on the sarcasm just a little bit," Nathan says, exaggerating the 'just', "you'll slightly be likeable."

Really now? I turn to Nathan with a complacent grin on my face.

"Then before you scold me about my personality, do something about your fashion sense." I scoff, eyeing Nathan's sickly, bright, Hawaiian shirt with a pink vest underneath and baggy, neon-green, board shorts. *Even if he's not my roommate anymore, this guy never changes.* I sigh in relief as my grin widens. *We're in the middle of autumn, you know?* But then again, I guess that bear has enough body hair to account for that. "Though, seeing that it hasn't changed for the past two years, it might be a lost cause."

I pull out a plastic bag hiding in the depths of my webbed locker and drop the blood-filled syringe into it. The name, 'Deianira D. Lobos' prints against the white nylon as I write her title with a small, balled-point pen. My punctured hands tremble as I struggle to hold the thin brass material, and I curse under my breath while walking to the oval desk of tightly strapped, black and white uniforms.

A wavering smile lifts on the Caretaker's face as they take the bag as the deposit, and I'm determined not to return it. My eyes run over the steel baton and spray, in a small case hanging upon their hips, and my frown deepens. *Like you're afraid of us.*

Nathan's high-pitched manly cries reach my ears, and my head cranes in annoyance as he pouts at me.

"What's wrong with my fashion?" he asks dumbfoundedly. "My little girl loves this style!"

A smirk dresses my lips as I squeeze my arm. "It looks like my personality stays."

Nathan cringes in disgust as he turns away from me. "Then don't blame me if someone gets hurt because of you!"

"I thought you were my only friend?"

A groan escapes Nathan's mouth as a smile plasters on my face.

"I give up," he surrenders, a light grin lifting his walnut cheeks.

Nathan's head cocks in curiosity, as cheers emanate throughout the room and the TV booms throughout the lobby. Another werewolf is fighting Battle Royale, one of the worst games made in Silver Rank – a fight to the death.

Nathan's large hand slaps my back, and I jolt in surprise as an enormous grin pins onto his face. "Feeling nostalgic? Why not give it another go?"

My nails pull at my sleeves as I remove my sights from the screen. "It won't be the same." *The thrill, the adrenaline, all of it has vanished once I'd gone over the wall. Who was I to step in all that glory? Plus, my time is long gone.*

"Come on. It's been months, don't chicken out." Nathan drags, jabbing me in the chest. "Or I'll simply do it for you."

"Wait, Nathan-"

Nathan winks as he sprints across the milk tiles and towards the roulette connected to the stadium. My branched legs rush after him, but his are longer, and he disappears to the side of the TV room behind blank walls. Nathan's shirt wrinkles in my hands as I attempt to pull his body back, but from the bulk of muscle he holds, he stands firmly in place, not even flinching.

Sweat pours down my frame as the bell to commence the games roll. My heart drums against my chest as I clutch my punctured hand from trembling even further. My eyelids close. Will it be a fight for my life, the taming of a beast, or will I have to succumb to my carnivorous instincts in order to survive? Scarlet trails down my chin as my canines pierce my lip. *Anything but that.*

The roll halts and a paper ticket slides out of the machine. My eyes don't dare to waver.

The hunt.

"Isn't my luck something, huh?" Nathan exclaims, as the deep scar slashed across his nose gleams in the lobby's light.

A sigh of relief escapes my mouth, and I lick the drops of blood falling from my lip.

"I didn't ask for it," I say, snatching the ticket as I walk past the werewolves jumping at the conflict on screen.

"What about my 'thank you'?"

"Buy new clothes, and maybe I'll consider it."

I spin towards Nathan with my eyes glistening at his boisterous frame.

"Not in a thousand years, pal!" Nathan shouts with a grin slapping across his face.

"Then there you have it. Later, Nathan," I say, flaunting the thin paper sheet in the air.

I head up the grand staircase, elevated by the Caretakers' desk, and stroll across the open corridor overlooking the three communal areas to head to my room. As I walk across the aisle, passing the other boys' door numbers, I stop in my tracks as I get a concerned glance from the werewolf staying next door.

My bedroom door hangs wide open and whiffs of blood oozes from the inside. A first aid kit, with a pack of fish blood poking from it, lies against the carpet with torn bandages unravelled beside it. Jay perches on the ladder leading to the top bunk, and his maroon eyes bear into me as I walk in.

"They really did a number on you," I comment, passing his scarred body holding deeper gashes than the previous ones before.

Jay grunts as he acknowledges my existence and continues to wrap the thin bandages around his shaved knuckles.

"Nothing I couldn't handle," he retorts.

I give a dry laugh as I lean against my desk. "Is looking miserable a new way to insult the weak?" I question.

A fierce glare penetrates my back as I insert my battle ticket into the picture book I own of The Outside World.

"But seriously, regenerating after three fights, are you that eager to go to hell?" I ask, turning to his beaten-up figure. His ribs are evident against his beige skin, slightly hollowed cheeks glue against his once handsome face, and his frame is smaller, much smaller than before. *This stupid child isn't taking care of his health either.* "Want me to kiss it better?"

"In your dreams."

A subtle smile graces my lips and soon shifts into a frown. The blemishes and scars shrouding Jay's body, from his sandy cheeks to his sculpted stomach, is a true display of the violence occurring behind closed doors. *Yet, we don't have a choice.* Fleeing may be an option, but Jay's torn frame already expressed he will do anything but that.

"Becoming 'Top Dog' isn't worth it, you know," I say, tracing my veiny fingers over Daniel's doodles sitting on the first page of my torn book. "Speaking from experience."

"It's none of your business," Jay states, attempting to pick up the pack of fish blood with shaky hands that could crumble at a second's notice.

"I'm telling you as your senior."

Jay eyes my figure cautiously as his eyes narrow. "Then spit it," he commands, "Last two weeks, where were you?"

My book shuts in my palms as I turn to Jay with the softest expression I can offer. "It's been two weeks. Why ask now-"

"You go over the wall?"

My eyes slightly widen as I part my lips, but the words stick in my throat. Desperate pleas infiltrate my head, for Jay to simply forget about what he asked, to not care about what I do, but Jay's brown pupils continue to pierce mine, and the silence only thickens. *Why all of a sudden?* Jay's glare deepens as my hand strokes the sharp line cutting across my jaw, and my hesitation tests his patience.

"I didn't," I confess.

Jay's furrow deepens as 'liar' must've been slapped across my forehead. His black eyes glare at me, and the longer they stay trained on my figure, the faster I fall into a bottomless pit fuelled with endless guilt. The harder it is to breathe, the harder it is to think, and the harder it is to break this suffocating silence.

"Then quit with your mindless shit," Jay finally says, putting the plastic pack to his mouth. "You're not going to get anything out of me unless you tell me the truth first."

I can't. My gaze doesn't remove from Jay's as he scowls at my figure.

"You're hiding something," he speculates, "and if it's what's out there, it won't be long till I find out."

Jay's eyes sink into his face as they shift into a sinister black. A devilish grin lifts his cheeks and I'm appalled by the fangs grinning at me, not belonging to a werewolf but a thirsty killer.

"Cuz we're roommates." he states, labelling a term with such a heavyweight of meaning. And even though this boy before me is much weaker than me, younger than me, and shorter than me, chills race down my spine. As his murderous intent sends needles extruding from my body and my tail eager to find solace between my legs, because that is an Alpha. The strongest amongst all wolves, the leaders of our Ancestors' pack, and if this ominous aura is the wrath of their anger, I'm not planning on biting off more than I can chew towards them in the future.

FINDERS, KEEPERS

I lean against the wooden shrine, and sigh as the snap of timber reverberates in my ears. Like a whinnying horse, the wolf altar creaks, but the expectancy of my body hitting the hard ground doesn't bother me as much as it should. Wolfsbane rushes down my throat as I bite the insides of my cheek, and my finger pushes against my temple as a groan leaves my lips. I was careless – my spot had been unknowingly claimed by that she-wolf, and it ticked me off. Yet, the longer my eyes settle on Maya's worn-out frame, intensively training by the large pond, the less I can find it in me to chase her out.

For her wolf is a complete work of art, cloaked in a pure silver undercoat with black strokes embellishing her mane. Along her white muzzle, cream fur runs from her button black nose to her rounded ears, complemented with a dash of brown. Though, what's astounding are her eyes. Her eyes when the light hit become orbs glossed in golden honey, fuelled with a pleasant sweetness as her soft gaze captivates mine.

Another sigh escapes my mouth.

"Can I join?" I ask, disregarding the awe welling inside of me every time my sights lie on her petite, furred face.

"O-of course," Maya stutters, fumbling over her words as she guides me to the riverbank as to where I should stand.

"Good." Daniel's leather necklace falls upon my chest, and a smirk reaches my lips as I remove my outer garments to reveal my sable bodysuit.

She's quite attentive, not fazed, causing a blush to spread against my cheeks as her eyes scan my body from head to toe once I position myself in a fighting stance before her.

"You ready?" I question, a sly smile raising my cheeks. Hair extends from my forearms, wrapping me in a tight sheet of extra muscle as a tail projects from my lower back. Daggers poke from my mouth and my pupils dilate, as my grey eyes flicker a piercing gold at Maya's frame.

She nods.

A low cackle leaves my black lips and my tail whips against the ground. "Then come at me."

A roar escapes Maya's muzzle as she lunges towards me and swipes frantically at my figure. Her mouth tightly clamps as she dances around me, waving her arms as if she's catching flies. A frown reaches my face, and my brows knit together as I hesitantly step back. *What are you, a cat?* She has the speed, I'll give her that, but the usage of her arms is close to none, and you want me to believe you can survive in a fight?

A wolfy grin smears on Maya's face as her nails scratch at my wrist. She seeks to gain a strike at my head as her sharp fur scratches against my cheeks, but I crouch faster. Stretching her arm behind her back, her form collapses into the long blades of grass, and a long sigh leaves my lips.

"Is that your attempt as a werewolf?" I question, raising a brow as I revert her transformation into its human form.

Maya stares at me with watery eyes as I release my hold.

"I-I am a werewolf!" she exclaims, rubbing her eyes with dirt-filled hands as snot begs to drop from her buttoned nose.

"You won't even put a hare to shame; who are you kidding?"

Maya's head sinks to the floor as she turns away from me. "Sorry…"

Her cheeks are full of grime, and a small tear dribbles down her chin. Like a frightened fawn, her body shivers as she sobs quietly in the open field, and guilt drops to my stomach. *So, I'm the bad guy?*

I scratch the back of my neck and stoop to her trembling figure.

"Again. Stand up." I sigh, offering my large hand to her.

Maya ignores my help and shifts into a silver wolf before me. A growl erupts from her throat as she lengthens her nails, swiping at my chest, and I block it, extending her small hand within mine. She struggles in my grip once I position myself behind her, and my hold on her tightens as my breath fans against the black strokes speckled upon her ash fur.

"Swing straight and extend your hand like a propeller," I advise, stretching Maya's arm to align with her chest, "when battling, it's better to use your back leg for support. You have a tinier frame, so use your legs to your advantage as much as possible."

A burning heat rises from Maya's body, and her ears turn a blazing red as she reverts her transformation. I swiftly let go, distancing myself from her flustered frame, and she takes my withdrawal as an opportunity to shove my body into the pond. It's a shame she isn't strong enough though, as a squeak leaves her system once I sling

52

her over my shoulder, and she plummets into the cold water.

Bubbles pop over the small, rippling waves as rays of light outline its every motion. Five seconds turn into six, and ten seconds become eleven, but Maya still isn't rising to the surface. *Can she not swim? The pond isn't deep; I can stand in it.* My finger scratches against my forehead as I scan the glistening waters. *Then again, I'm a six-foot-tall giant, not a five-footer.* I squat beside the pond bed and wait for any sign of movement. If she doesn't come up in the next five seconds, I'll have to go in. *As much as I hate it, I'm not becoming a killer today.*

A hand shoots from the pond and grabs my arm as it pulls me within.

"Wai-"

Water fills my lungs, biting at my skin as the icy liquid devours me. A large grin glues on Maya's face as she circles effortlessly around me, and her small body shines like a ray of light in the crispy waters. My hand extends to her swimming figure, and I sink further into the deemed 'small' pond as my transformation sinks me like a rock.

"I am NOT a fan of those sneak attacks of yours!" I exclaim, hacking the water drowning my body as I reach the surface.

An angelic laugh caresses my ears as Maya's giggle, which's as smooth as velvet, showers me like a blessing.

"I'm sorry, I had to," Maya affirms, shoving a sly grin in my face, "Otherwise, I wouldn't be able to win."

My body shudders as the wind hits against my coal skin, and I glare at her.

"Well, it's also to get back at you for beating me all those times," she confesses.

"That was self-defence," I state, shaking the water out of my hair.

"I thought I was 'weaker than a hare'?"

"Fleas are just annoying as you too," I comment, her words becoming a blur.

Maya's wide, glistening eyes, with a tinge of gold, stare at me like an attention-seeking pup. Her dark, pink lips curve with every chuckle, revealing the light dimples pressing along the sides of her mouth. The raven strands, she is too unbothered to brush away, stick against her skin, exposing her light cream collarbone. And her soaked, V-neck bodysuit enhances her small curves, and bulges her melon-shaped chest. *Thank the Ancestors; the facility designed them to be black.*

"H-hey!"

My head shoots up to Maya's pouting face as crimson dusts my cheeks.

"But then again, that means me – a Top Dog, got beaten by a flea." I chuckle, combing my fingers through her silky, black strands. "Well done, on upgrading to fly status."

She narrows her eyes as she turns away from me, "I don't think flies can swim."

"Then you're a mosquito."

Maya sucks in her cheeks and puckers her lips. My eyebrows furrow at her distorted expression, and we look at each other for what seems to be a minute till her expression drops.

"It's a mosquito…" she explains.

My jaw aches and my stomach hurts. A chortle escapes from my mouth as my hand smacks against the ground. *That was pathetic.* Maya cuddles her knees in embarrassment as tears crystallise in her amber eyes. I tuck a strand of hair behind her ear and apologize, but my body fails me as a light snort escapes my lips and she scolds me. Though as she takes in my chuckling frame, a smile is evident behind her words as she registers the immense grin plastering on my face.

From then on, meeting Maya became a part of my schedule, and our time spent together would begin and end in the field before our Ancestor's shrine. As quickly as Maya came, trees stood stark naked within the chilled air, and small, white flurries descended from the cerulean blue sky. Two days turned into one week, and two weeks turned into three months, as every day we would train, chat, and mess around till we got tired of the other's company – which we never did. Occasionally, we'd skip our night routine, camping underneath the dark-painted canvas, embroidered with polished gems, showering its angelic luminescence onto our faces. Whenever we had jobs to do, lies would disperse from our lips like a part of our second nature as if bewitched by a spell that refused to pull us apart. The more we met, the more curiosity welled within my system – Maya's likes, her dislikes, her friends, her family, the reason she'd come here, I had a greediness to find out more about her. Every time her image popped in my mind, the eagerness to gaze at her endearing form, run my fingers through her silky hair, embrace her small body in my arms, and bury myself in her alluring, sweet scent took control of me. Her favourite colour, her favourite food, her favourite drink, her brother, I'd learned it all, but I wanted more.

Maya hums as the sun's rays brush against her face. Like a lucky charm, the days are always this bright, and the sky so clear every time she appears. For when our sights contain one another, her eyes will glisten more radiantly than the beaming rays beating down on our faces on a sunny day.

Maya's head droops to the edge of the bank as she stares up at me with a frown placed upon her small face. "I'm going to say something weird."

A chuckle leaves my mouth as I return her glance.

"You don't say?" I tease, leaning against Maya's back on the pond bed as her hair falls against my face, "Well, I can't say I expect anything sane, from someone who follows me like a pup constantly into this shit-smelling place without complaining."

Maya's face turns beet red as she turns towards me, shoving my body against the floor, "That's because I like it here-"

"You like it?"

A sly grin slaps onto my face as I get up from the ground and pinch Maya's plump, red cheeks. "Liar."

She wiggles in her spot, attempting to pry my hands off and pouts.

"I-I can move freely!" she shouts in annoyance.

"I thought you said you had something weird you wanted to say?" I ask, and she glares at me as my smile widens, "So, your real reason is?"

"I-" Maya twirls her raven tresses along her fingertips as her head sinks to the floor. Her eyes run along the ripples of water as she pinches her fingers and furrows her brows. "It's nothing. Forget it."

"Now I'm curious." My arm enlarges and wraps around Maya's neck as she jolts from my touch.

"Hey-"

"I thought I told you how to escape a person's clutch." I muse, a smirk dressing my lips as the hairs on my transformed arm prick against Maya's skin. "Or are my words *that* insignificant?"

Maya turns to me with her mouth agape as she flushes red, "I-"

"10 seconds."

"Gabriel, I can't-"

"1."

"I don't-"

"You don't remember?" My eyes light up as Maya forcibly attempts to wiggle out of my chokehold, "2."

"Gabriel," she draws out, pushing her small body against mine as she twists and turns.

"3."

"I'll tell you, I'll tell you."

"4."

"Gabriel!" Maya's head falls in my hold as she pouts at me while softly murmuring, "I'll tell you, so let me go."

Hair retracts into my arm, and a smug grin slaps onto my face as Maya sticks her tongue out at me. She takes in my figure for a moment, then clamps her jaw. Her mouth opens, and she sucks in a deep breath as she stares at me intently with quivering brown eyes. "It's just…" she exhales deeply as she holds a hand against her chest. "I like you."

My body stills as the words pass from her mouth. My lips quiver, but there's a reluctance to the response 'I like you too.' A horrible guilt streams through me, and my stomach throbs as knives pierce through my chest. My eyelids tightly close, and my jaw clamps. *I can't say it.*

Maya entangles her fingers with mine as crimson engulfs her body to the tips of her ears. "It's a bit sudden, but… if it's you, I want to be-"

Mates. Bonded pairs that never tear away from each other even during life and death. The dignity of only having one partner in their entire life, being part of a wolf's pride – a matter chosen wisely. I remove my hand and get up from beside her as Maya's eyebrows tilt into a frown. The world darkens as the scenery, her face, and her words, turn into thick chains wrapping around my body.

"I'm sorry, I can't," I say, as my nails dig into my palms.

Why? It's scribbled all over her face, like an abandoned puppy searching for its lost owner. Yet, in those few seconds of the confession, it all came back to me. The time in this facility, the countless torture of my hard work, the pain I'd gone through, I'm doing it all for Daniel. *How can mere months make me forget about my top priority? The only existence that made me make this decision in the first place?* My eyes land on Maya's crumbling figure on the verge of tears for the last time, and I make my way down the concrete staircase, refusing to look back. If I did, those large, shimmering orbs will catch me in a trance, and everything I'd sacrificed myself for Daniel's sake, would've truly been forgotten.

I storm into the facility, overlooking its blinding white walls, and dash through the lobby's corridor. Swinging my fists as I run, my lungs cry for air, and my legs sink like lead as the guilt of the rejection churns in my head. Maya's face, her scent, her touch, they aren't leaving! Though, as if they'll leave without a trace after all the months we'd spent together. I sigh as I open my bedroom door, and my body freezes.

Chains, steel blades, firearms, and weapons that shouldn't belong to a werewolf, litter the floor in a disarray. I tiptoe my way across the disorderly room and kick a can of pepper spray with the label 'Caretaker' written on it. A pungent odor unleashes from the bottle as I pick it up, and it clatters to the ground as my arm shoots to my nose. I plop myself onto the bottom bunk as I overlook the steel items of all shapes and sizes sprawled across the floor, and a groan escapes my lips. *This is a mess.* A smoky scent hits the back of my throat, and I look up towards the fur coat dangling along the edges of Jay's bed. *A familiar scent.* I sniff it further as a powerful, toxic, sweet odour digs into my nostrils, and I stop. *There's also a scent of wolf.* My hands tug at the fabric as my eyes widen. *It's clothing from a Beast Tamer.*

"The hell are you doing!?" Jay growls, yanking the fur coat out of my hands. "Who asked you to put your shitty hands on my stuff?"

My heart sinks as my stomach turns. It's more a statement than a question.

"You're planning to go over the wall," I mumble, my eyes sternly locking onto Jay's frame while he buttons his shirt as if he'd come over in a rush.

"So?"

"Don't."

Pain tears at my skin, reliving the moment as Dean's cigarette burn enlightens against my chest.

My jaw clenches as anger flares in my pupils. *Listen to me.*

"Don't tell me what to do." he hisses.

My claws are eager to lunge at his short frame, plummet his body into the floor and keep him in place, but I refrain.

"Jay, you don't know what's out there!" I shout, my grey hues pleading for his withdrawal.

"Then you tellin' me?" he asks, and my mouth opens with the words lingering upon my tongue. "Move."

"No."

My body slams into the metal of the bunk bed as Jay towers over me. Pain spirals up my spine, but compared to the anger welling inside of me, it's only slight.

"Move!" Jay snaps, canines cracking his jaw as his eyes thrust into his head.

"Is rejection too hard for you to understand? I said no." I snarl as ears shoot from my scalp, and thorned hairs scatter across my skin.

64

"Then if words don't get to you, I'll give it to you straight."

Stings strike into my lower back as Jay hurls me into the ground. His sinister, onyx eyes glower deeply into my yellow pupils as his claws seep into my shirt, and his hot breath fans against my face. "Quit acting like you're bigger than me. Ever since I got here, you've been spouting shit non-stop, 'don't do this, don't do that.' You're only two years older than me, quit acting like a big shot; it pisses me off!"

A shuddering roar emits from his inked lips as he slings me to the side with a face of an enraged beast. My nails scratch at the carpet as I hold myself back from unleashing my rage.

"Last time I checked, there wasn't anything wrong with trying to keep someone safe, Jay!" I spit, blaring my fangs at his grotesque figure. "You can't escape this place!"

Jay's twisted figure smirks at me as he weighs his black talons against the room's hanging white light, flickering against his touch, "Who said I was escaping?"

My mouth drops as my claws lift from the floor's fabric. "Then, what the hell are you doing?"

Jay's mane sinks into his skin, and his nails retract as he turns away from me, "It's none of your business."

I scoff as a growl rumbles within my chest. "Acting like a brat seems like one of your strong points. Especially if you can't even listen to some simple advice."

Jay's canines protrude from his gums as his eyes roar like a serpent entangling its prey, choking it into the depth of hell within its grasp, as he confines me within his view.

"Say that again; I dare you." he growls as his throat rumbles with the intenseness of his voice.

Cold sweat drips from my frame as pins and needles stream through my hands and legs. My eyes stick to Jay's threatening gaze, as I force down the hoarse breaths desperate to protrude from my lips.

Bang!

My head snaps to the front door.

"Lights out! In your rooms!" The Caretaker shouts, banging the alloy with a metal baton.

A sigh of relief escapes my system as Jay regresses his transformation and his temper cools. He picks up the littered items strewn across the floor and stuffs them into a grey backpack, sitting atop his bed, as he snarls.

"Don't even think of stopping me," he says, grabbing the fur coat and shoving it into his rucksack.

"I won't." I retort, closing my eyes. *I won't stop you.* A long breath treads my lips as my fur retracts into my skin, and I calm my enraged heart. "But that's only if you let me come with you."

Jay's eyes bear into my long frame as I refuse to flinch under his strong gaze. *It's either that.* My grey eyes flicker a piercing gold as I grip onto the bed's steel ladder. *Or I deal with you myself, Jay.*

KANYA

My thin shirt crumples in my grasp as sweat pours down my skin. Slices of air shred my throat as hoarse coughs erupt from my mouth, and heat flushes against my face as a string of saliva crawls down my lips. *Where are you?* My thighs burn as I drop down the lobby's staircase and bolt towards the Girls' dorms with my sandals squeaking against the tiles.

Static noise blares from the T.V screens, as canted posters of today's 'Wolf Fight' curtains the previously collaged walls. A wild and un-mannerly cheer erupts from the werewolves' bodies, as lines of slang and curses protrude from their inked lips. Feeling no shame, unaware, and performing like today, is no different than yesterday.

Blood trickles down my nose as I face plant into the ground. My eyes follow the sticky essence plastered to the floor as I slump against the icy tiles. *Where is she?* A groan escapes my lips as I put my hand to my nose and attempt to ease the stings biting at my face.

"H-hey, you!" I cry, receiving a nasty glare from a brunette as she squints at my fallen figure.

Smears of blood stain my white shirt as I wipe the drops of sweat falling from my frame. Air saturates my lungs as I take a deep breath, and I gradually find the strength to stand straight before her.

"Do you know a girl named Maya?" I ask, my eyes locking onto her baffled ones. The roof of my mouth screeches for a cold liquid to rush down my throat, yet my eyes gleam with hopefulness. *I want to apologise.*

The girl puts a finger to her temple as her brow creases, "Maya? Who- Are you sure you didn't mistake it for a boy's name, like Milo, or something?"

My jaw grits.

"Do you think I'd ask if I did? Can't you check for me? Maybe you're mistaken?"

A murky-brown flickers within the girl's pupils as she bares her fangs. *Shit.* Her dainty fingernails dig into my collar, and a deep growl rumbles from her throat, "I've been here for three years. I can assure you there's no wolf here called Maya, *mate.*"

My body jerks back as she shoves past me and vanishes through the Girls dorm's salmon, glass door, and a sigh escapes my lips. My head drops to my knees as I squat to the floor. *Alphas are such short-tempered wolves, and such a pain to deal with; can't even take a single question.* Furthermore, this is the gazillionth time I've asked for her. The shrine, the Canteen, the T.V room, the lockers, I've looked everywhere!

Werewolves stroll past me as they head to watch the ongoing matches with grinning faces and chatty remarks. Numerous times I've asked whether they know where Maya is, and it was those same quizzical expressions, the same, 'Who are you talking about?' the repetition was constant – it doesn't make sense. *Why does nobody know her, except for me?*

I position myself upright and step through the baby pink doorway. Various stares penetrate my back as I observe the numbers decorating the girls' doors. *147,148,149,150.* An amber doorway dims my view, and a groan leaves my lips. Blasting the door wide open till its hinges slam against the ground will be sensational, but a dozen she-wolves have their claws unsheathed and canines glistening at my figure, and I'm not planning on dying today.

My knuckle strikes the wood, and as the surface taps against my hand, I fall forward. Carpet slams into my face, and a scowl crosses my features as the door flings open with blue eyes gleaming in amusement.

"Been a while since you decided to pay me a visit." Oliver snickers, extending her hand to my sprawled figure. "Though, to be fairly honest, I was expecting your corpse to be the last memory I had of you. I'm glad to see you alive and well, *Gabe.*"

Trickles of blood drip down her pale hand as I slap it away with a snarl erupting from my throat. "That makes one of us."

Her smile widens, as bright as the blond tresses falling upon her forehead, as I stand up with golden eyes glowering at her smirking frame. *That witch, to have the nerve to act innocent, after all you've done.*

"I see you haven't changed; how unfortunate." Oliver sighs, closing the door behind me. She picks up a purple handkerchief sitting at her desk and turns to me, "So, how can I help you?"

I cringe in disgust as she licks the laps of blood dripping from her half-gloved hand. Her phantom blue pupils dig into mine as she dips the cloth into a bowl of water, containing a Wolfsbane stalk, and she dabs it against her wound – never removing her sights from me.

"Did you know, tolerating less than ten percent of the liquid from Wolfsbane fastens our regeneration?" Oliver asks, removing the cloth and revealing a white, bony hand that no longer had cuts upon it, as if there were no wounds in the first place.

"I don't care." I blankly state, as she chuckles quietly whilst placing her handkerchief on her wooden desk.

Dust scatters upon her slender form as her tall bookshelves slump against the walls. Informative books, written by the witch herself, fill their large compartments, whether it be for good or her malicious intentions – a different story altogether. Her furniture, built of oak wood, brought a dark, gothic atmosphere to her quarters, and it doesn't matter if it's day outside; once Oliver's blinds draw close, you'll be swallowed in a sombre darkness you can't escape from. *Perfect for a witch of her calibre.* As it isn't a room – it's an experimentation lab, where the worst of her ideas come to fruition. Having the only thing classifying it as a bedroom being the small bed tucked in the corner, illuminated by her blue lamp.

"Then, may I ask what you'd like of me?" Oliver asks, picking up an open book she began reading before catching my scent at the front door.

I grit my teeth as she flips a page. *She's playing with me, and she's enjoying that.* That smile, visible against the pages, holds no regrets of sending me to venture beyond the wall, and the mere thought causes anger to swell in my chest. Though she knew Daniel, and the last thing I need is to be threatened if I attempt to claw the smirk off her face right now.

I groan in irritation as my hands clap against my face. "Tell me everything you know about a werewolf named Maya."

Oliver raises her eyebrows as she peeks over the pages of her book.

"You spent all your time with a she-wolf, hm?" she comments, "Am I not good enough for you?"

"Far from it."

"I see," she says, gently placing the book onto her desk as she searches through the sea of volumes, she has about the Wolf Foundation, sitting upon the bookshelves.

"Rank?" Oliver questions, caressing the bleached covers encasing the novels.

"Bronze," I answer, as Oliver takes out books one by one.

"Age?"

"18."

"Hair colour and length?"

"Black, waist-length."

"And nobody knew her?"

Oliver's blue eyes seep into my still figure as she cradles a large book, reading '2003 records' within her large, gloved hands.

"Yeah," I mumble.

Oliver stares at the volume, then looks back at me. My chest tightens as her raven-clothed form places the book carefully upon her oak desk.

"Is this the wolf you're looking for?" she asks, peering at me as she keeps the records open with a brown pen.

A blank page stares at me, with solely little detail on the other, and I squint to get a better look at the sheets of white paper lined with short, black notes. *Such small and cursive handwriting, how could I possibly-*

The book slams close before I can get a gist of what the text writes, and I glare at Oliver's chuckling frame.

"Whoops," Oliver snickers, wiping her thumb across the hardcover's lilac casing, "I believe information comes with a price. Surely, you haven't forgotten that have you?"

I growl, my sanity draining every time she opens her mouth. *Was sending me to the depths of hell not enough for you!? If I knew your true colours from the start, the last thing I'll be doing is asking for your help.*

I sigh as my nails dig into my palms. "I'll give you information about Deianira, so give me the file."

A large grin slaps across Oliver's square face, and she rests her hand underneath her chin.

"I figured we'd understand each other," she says, sliding the file towards me.

The volume weighs in my hands as I scan the pages. A small picture of a black, short-haired female lies embedded between the sheets, and as I scoop it out, those glossy, honey, brown eyes become recognisable as Maya's.

"Is this wolf…interesting to you?" Oliver asks, staring at how gently I'm holding the picture. A sigh escapes her lips as she fiddles with the strands falling atop her round glasses. "I'd think it thoroughly if I were you. Unless you want to be one of 'their' many toys." she adds, a smirk painting her lips. "For you, however, it may not seem that bad."

My face scrunches in confusion, "What are you saying? Maya's-"

"First, it's not Maya. It's Kanya." Oliver affirms, sliding her finger along the rim of the page to the dreadful, cursive writing that reads, *'Werewolf no#237 Kanya Vigolfr'.* "Maya is a fake name that I'm guessing she created herself."

My fingers run cold as the book I'm holding suddenly feels foreign.

"Second," Oliver continues, combing her hands through the scratches engraved against her half-shaved head, "I know of your dislike towards me-"

"Hate. I hate you." I correct, glaring at those phantom, dark-blue hues.

"Right," she says, a small smile lifting her lips. "But listen, I'm telling you this for your own sake, Gabriel."

Oliver closes in on me as she presses her cold hands onto my arms. Her breath tingles against my skin as a frown contorts her sly face.

"That girl isn't who you think she is. Stay away from her."

LUPERCALIA

I trudge across the broad, barren terrain like a broken machine as goosebumps pop against my brown skin. Cold air snakes its way into my sandals, numbing my toes as they weigh into the worn asphalt with a heavyweight bearing upon my shoulders. The more my footsteps echo along this quiet road, the heavier my body becomes. *How many minutes has it been since I passed the gateway?* An eerie chill runs down my spine as neon toy houses gape at my stick figure.

White picket fences sit on the rims of the houses' freshly cut gardens, as lifeless gnomes lie stashed away from the road's view inside of them. Roses bloom within their beds, wrapping their jagged thorns around newly grown hedges, as they pick at the growing shrubs, preventing them from reaching the raven sky and spreading their leaves for comfort. Bright red apples glisten in the silver light as if made of pure glass, and they are so perfectly rounded and radiant, it's as if you were to bite into them - a cold air will brush your lips as you stare blankly at its hollow inside. A suffocating tightness clutches my chest, and I peer at the unstained windows glistening in the moonlight's rays. Not a single light filters through their glass frames despite the houses' countless numbers, as if this were a ghost town.

My heavy breathing sounds in my ears as drums and laughter echo behind the large, grey walls. Songs and cheer emit from the humans' cries as the celebration of Lupercalia, the day the humans won the war, continues onward. Within the starry lights, Kirkos' emblem - a half-headed wolf, howling at the stars atop the crescent moon, upon blue, red, and grey flags, props on thick sticks along the large slabs of stone as they mark the symbol of the humans' honour.

My upper lip curls as my nose wrinkles. The mere sight is making me sick to my stomach. "Jay, this is not-"

"If you're gonna tell me to go back, keep your mouth shut."

My head drops to the floor as my eyes scan Jay's figure. His black boots stomp against the gravel as a low growl erupts from his throat. Clangs rattle in his backpack as it clings on his shoulders once he paces to the market's entrance. The fluffy collar wrapped around his neck, creases every time the bag's leather straps fall to his arms, and by the time we reach halfway to the market, the Beast Tamer's coat is a scrunched bundle of fluff - equivalent to a cat's hairball. *What does this small, malnourished child think he can do?* Air exhales from my nose as a groan escapes my lips.

"What!?" Jay snaps as he spins towards me.

"We're on the road, and the vans-"

"I'm not blind, jack-ass!" Jay barks, taking me aback as a puzzling expression finds its way onto my face, "They come out every hour, and we got ten minutes. So, if you don't wanna die, cut with the useless shit and keep walking."

My fingers crack underneath the glistening light, my claws begging to be unsheathed, as my canines stop growing an inch shorter from piercing my lips. *Ha. Is this a new way pups treat their seniors that I somehow wasn't aware of? This kid is really testing my patience.* I tag along silently before a single word escaping my mouth permits mine or Jay's demise.

Fluorescent lights beam behind the wall, uplifting the vigorous cheers directed at the humans' festival. Vibrant moon-shaped lanterns decorate the sky, as strings of light fall from the edges of the walls into the bustling market. Roasted meat, sautéed vegetables, chilled desserts; various aromas land on the tip of my tongue, sliding down the back of my throat and settling against my chest. Yet the most pungent, making my stomach turn, is the humans' stifling scent overflowing into my nostrils. Jay jerks forward as I hit into his back, and an un-describable scowl reaches on his face.

Four werewolves stand chatting at the entrance with large, radio collars marking their duty and identity. Jay's fur coat falls to the floor, revealing his black, zipper jacket and hoodie, and he hastily digs through his rucksack. *Does he finally realise this is a mistake?* My eyes run over the rowdy guards not taking their jobs seriously. *Those werewolves are unmistakably Alphas; fighting them will be our loss.*

A can of wolfsbane spray hits the edge of my shoe as Jay glowers at me.

"Spray it." he commands, throwing a thick cloth at my face.

My brows furrow as a concerned smile presses against my lips. *You can't be serious-*

"Spray it!"

A swirling storm of darkness eradicates my morality, as Jay's glare sends chill after chill spiraling down my spine. *How long did he plan for this? Instead of wishing to explore The Outside World, seeing its wonders, aweing at its beauty, was he researching the facility the whole time? But for what?* A cold sweat runs down my brow as I push the top of the Caretakers can and spray that horrid, bitter odour, gushing from its nozzle, into the red cloth. Chains clatter against the ground as Jay wraps them around his arms, and his stolen fur coat slings onto his back, together with his rucksack as he dashes towards the werewolves swinging the heavy metal in his hands.

"You're not actually going to-"

Before the words leave my mouth, a high yelp resounds before the market as Jay batters the large chain against a werewolf's head. Growls erupt from the werewolves' throat as the image of their squirming comrade, plastered against the concrete, wells within their view. I curse under my breath as Jay weighs his feet into the victim's face and eyes the wolf guards surrounding him, with a chill sending icicles piercing at my chest. Sweat runs down my brow, and I clutch the cloth tightly in my grasp. *It'll only be seconds till they hunt me down too.*

A grunt leaves one of the wolf guards as my foot slams into his back, and the revolting cloth presses onto his face. Nails scrape at my dead skin as he struggles in my hold, and every twist and turn he makes is a fight for his life. Sweat pours down his skin as muffled cries burst from his mouth, making the toxins flow faster into his body. My eyes narrow as I burrow my head into the crook of his neck. *I'm*

84

sorry. Drool drips from the cloth onto his flannel shirt and scarf as his eyelids close. A muscular weight drops in my hands, and his legs give way as his hands drag along his sides. We both bask in an unnerving silence, and I rest his body upon the dreary road as I drape his white shawl over my shoulders. A harsh battle cry rings in my ears, and my neck snaps as my eyes widen.

Bear claws lunge at my figure as the companion of the beaten wolf guard jumps at me, barking multiple curses at my frame. Her weight smashes into the concrete as she swipes at my face with a sneer painted on hers. Blood dribbles down my nose as my heel crashes into her face, and her nails dig into my ankles. *Damn it.* I attempt to wiggle my legs out of her grasp, but her claws dig deeper, diving into my flesh, and finding their way to my muscles. A groan leaves my lips as the pain jolts up my leg, and I scratch at her refusing to lose a limb. Her face twists in agony as she releases her grasp, and she pulls against her nape with choked screams. Chains coil around her neck as her body slams into the slabs of rock once Jay drags her body against the road.

"What you waitin' for?" Jay snaps, scorning my bleeding physique, "Do it."

My fangs bare at his words as my hands brush my ankle. I resistantly stand up and stumble towards the bickering female hauling obscene curses at my frame. The befoul cloth attaches to her face, and it suffocates her as she thrashes against the icy floor. My brows furrow as her body twitches, gradually coming to a stop, and her eyes roll to the back of her head as saliva dribbles down her chin. *'They're just unconscious.'* I remind myself. Though as I take in the defeated werewolves' still figures, nothing but guilt fills my system. *We're just fulfilling our jobs as the humans' pets; they've done nothing wrong. So, who am I to do this to them?*

My eyes glance at Jay swinging an electric leash around the last wolf's collarbone as he brings them to their knees. Their writhing form sits at his feet, puny and pale. If Jay's shimmering, black eyes weren't glaring at the wolf guard within the dark of the night, I would've mistaken his ruthlessness for a Gladiator's. Jay approaches each fallen werewolf, and tampers with their black collars as he turns their broadcasting off, and I don't know what concerns me most - his thoughts of researching this, or the amount of time he's spent researching his own kind.

A grunt leaves my lips as I drop the last wolf guard behind a large, wheeled bin. The black crate covers their body as I glimpse at the market's entrance for any sign of movement. *Luckily, there's none.*

I trot behind Jay as we walk into the market, like two human guests disguised in segments of their clothing. Human voices buzz within our ears as I tug further on the white shawl, concealing my collar. My nails dig further into the cloth as my fingers tremble. The humans' scent is much stronger now, coating my body like thick oil as it swallows me into the ground. Bright smiles caress the humans' faces, concealing the bitter truths hidden underneath their muddy masks. My gaze lowers as it sets on Jay's cool and poised physique. It's as if here is the place he belongs. Every time my grey eyes skim his figure, his posture's upright and smug, with ignorance lacing his features, as he effortlessly strolls through the territory of a species that detained us.

"You're a wolf, right?"

My head spins frantically as my eyes skim the tents of various colours surrounding us.

A grey wolf with salty tears lining its eyes whimpers as it scratches at the bars of a small, steel cage underneath a dark, blue tent. Wounds scatter across its half-shaved body, revealing its bright, pink skin as it shivers underneath the metallic glint.

"Help me, please." It pleads, stuffing its muzzle through the tightly spaced bars. "They're going to murder me! They're going to hang-"

A high yelp escapes the canine's muzzle as its cage screeches across the gravel. Urine secretes onto the pavement as the cage tilts upside down, rattling with the connection of the wolf's trembling body.

"You don't know when to stop barking, do you!?" A Gladiator bellows, stomping on the prison locking the blemished wolf. "What's it gonna take to keep your mouth shut, huh!?"

The Gladiator's fiery dark hues look up at me, and my heart escalates up my throat.

"Got a problem?" The Gladiator growls, kicking the cage upright.

Water drips from the wolf's eyes, dissolving into patches of crimson within its matted fur as it whines, "You're a wolf, right?"

My teeth rub against each other as my chest tightens.

"Help me." It begs as my eyes lock onto its squashed figure, and I barely suffice a swallow.

I-

A punch lands in my gut and I double over in pain. Black eyes loom over me as they disdain my figure, and a scowl plasters on my lips.

"Do I look like a damn tour guide to you?" Jay snarls, twisting his knuckles further into my abdomen, "If you want to be breathing by the time you get back, quit stalling. It's not your first time."

My jaw grits as a grunt escapes my throat. The cramped werewolf's cries grow louder as I set my sights on the market. Stalls pass us by as my body rushes with sparks of adrenaline - to hurry and go, to get out of this place. Yet the further we enter, the fainter the humans' scent, and the stronger the wolves' scent becomes.

Raw meat strings from merchant shops with the chanting of thighs, breasts, ribs, and various red meats escaping from the merchants' mouths. A, B, and O labels, protrude from the stock displayed as laps of blood drip onto the flooring. Wolf heads sit at the front of stores with high, price tags clipped to their ears, as fur coats dangle at the back of accessory shops. Claws and fangs, remodeled into jewelry, exhibit their beauty to human-passerby as human children ogle at their metallic glint. In the corner of small shops, famished wolves aggravatingly bite on steel bars capturing them, as the sign *'Live Werewolf'* sits beside them.

My hand clutches my nose as the scent of wolf emanates from this place. Acid escalates up my throat, and nausea swirls in my stomach as the smell of death penetrates my nostrils. The cries of pain and anger are deafening - like deathly hollows gnawing at my soul.

Scratching at my chest, a white arch, with blue ribbons dropping from the ceiling, towers over our bodies as we enter The Beast Tamers' Paradise. An overpowering wolf stench gushes from the abode as it welcomes us, and my lungs turn blue. Crimson liquid streams from milk fountains as they fill Beast

Tamers' diamond glasses to the brim. Platters encased with chunks of red meat sit on long, white, dining tables, overlayed with the most gruesome décor: tails, nails, eyes. Bile escalates my throat and it's hard to swallow.

"Hey," I say, grasping Jay's shoulder as the colour drains from my face, "I don't know what you want, but it's not here."

My grip on his broad build tightens as he stares at me burping into my palm.

"I didn't ask for your opinion." he states, slapping my hand away and walking towards the centre of the hall as his brows furrow.

Of course, it's affecting him; Jay is a werewolf too! But is what he's here for, in the scent of death, really worth it?

"Jay!" I shout as Jay turns away, ignoring my calls.

I grumble in frustration as I look back. *That boy is such a stubborn-*

A reptilian green meets my quivering pupils, and the urge to break into tears wells within me.

"Jay, we should go back-"

My body lurches forward as Jay's hot breath flushes against my face and his nails sink into my collar.

"I should've just left you!" he snarls as a pair of furred arms wrap themselves around the both of us which causes him to flinch.

"Go back? Isn't the party just starting, boys?" Dean coos, downing a cup of thick, red fluid swirling within a wine glass. "Come, come. I'll show you around. It's only natural since you look *new* here."

Goosebumps prick against my skin as my body shivers uncontrollably once Dean releases her hold on the both of us. Jay witnesses the fear pulsating in my eyes, and for a second, he too feels afraid.

"But before that," Dean says, twisting her body with a platter of red meat. "Why not give our treats a try? Missing out on such a delicacy is simply taboo in this estate. You're not going to pass the offer, are you?"

The odour emitting from the dish makes my stomach clamber up my throat. It pulsates against the plate the closer Dean pushes it towards us, and the more she does, the further I step back. My head turns.

"I-… we don't have much of an appetite." I stammer, pulling myself away from the hallucinations dancing in my vision.

"Shame," Dean says, staring dismally at the cooked meat, "and I was sure you were eager to view our goods, as well."

A grin plasters on her face as she notes Jay's widening eyes.

Jay's hand hesitantly reaches out to the thick, lengthy pieces of meat laid out in front of him as a gulp echoes in his throat. The meat presses against his mouth as black flakes rub against his lip. His tongue hesitantly leaves his mouth, and he lets the meat's taste dissolve beneath his pink muscle till his teeth chomps onto the piece of fat. Ripping the flesh from the bone, Jay chews slowly as sweat drips down his cheeks and oil smears against his lips. His temples furrow.

"Tasty, isn't it?" Dean beams, placing the plate back onto the table.

Jay nods as I stare at him in disbelief. *You- What the hell?* My brows turn upright as I take a step back away from him. *You just ate a wolf! Your own kind!*

Jay retches and kicks the ball of chewed meat underneath the table as Dean turns her back. He slams his hand onto the wooden counter as a strangled cry erupts from his throat, and what I can't distinguish from a tear or a drop of sweat lines his bottom eyelid. His hand trembles across the table for water, but wolf blood and wolf meat are the only available items to digest.

"As expected of our most talented butchers who sell their works of art in Kirkos' best-selling auction," Dean chimes, pointing towards a grand building, with bright lights glimmering on black columns on the left side of the hall. She turns to our figures and smiles. "Want to take a look?"

Jay glowers at Dean as he nods falteringly. *Why!?* My hand yanks Jay back, but he shoves me aside and continues walking beside Dean. *To do this much, for what!?*

I move hesitantly beside them, the scents intoxicating, nausea wearing me out - Jay, wearing me out. *What happened to getting out alive, huh? Every step we take is one step closer to death!* My body flinches as we enter the side of the auction venue.

A rectangular box, the size of a human being, sits in the middle of the stage as a Beast Tamer draped in a top hat and fur coat steps into the spotlight. *'Beta'* in bold dances across the screen atop the podium as he pulls along a werewolf clad in heavy chains and scars stretching across his body. The audience ogles at the trembling male as the werewolf shies away from their piercing stares.

As the two make a stand-still, the owner fishes out a purple, liquid-filled syringe out of his pocket and stabs it into the tied werewolf. Ear-splitting cries erupt from the werewolf's system as his body's shoved into the wooden box. The door slams shut, subduing his effortless wails, and gapped lines are evident on the casing—his neck, forearms, torso, legs, and ankles.

The Beast Tamer wields a Butcher's axe mounted on his hip, and I close my eyes as sharp, broken screams leave the werewolf's mouth.

95

"Gimme a leg!" A person in the audience cries.

"The head!" Another shouts.

"I want the tail!"

The audience rages as the prices of each body part pings on screen. Blood seeps from the wooden box, coating the marble stage in a deadly crimson, and humans hurriedly reach for the red essence trickling from the podium as the werewolf's agonizing cries lie silenced by the rioting crowd - hungry for its flesh.

"Werewolves can be so lively, can't they?" Dean sighs, turning to us.

I close my eyes in an attempt to slow down my breathing. *Act normal.* Though the more the darkness consumes me, the faster the torturous exhibition of the werewolf's last moments replay at the back of my mind.

Jay clenches his hand into a fist as a vein pops against his temple. "Where's blood type O?"

"Are you interested?" Dean smiles, that same evil grin I've seen many times before, and my body shudders, "We have a special place for Omegas *too.*"

96

Behind the stage, the overpowering odour of faeces and Wolfsbane gushes from a small room. Its un-painted, oak door looms within its centre, as it stands as the entrance to small, wooden steps and tall, wooden beams reaching from the ground to the cracked ceiling. Lowly hung, pale, yellow lights flicker within the room, and underneath the dull light, blood-bathed werewolves litter the floor - some stationary - whilst others' chests heave drastically with metal bonds strapped to their bodies. Their tongues loll against the ground as manure clings onto their greasy coats with tags clipped onto their malnourished physiques. *Within a few hundred, a number's missing.* Small bones jam between their plaque, encased teeth, as stretched, scratch marks, and bite wounds decorate their faces. My nails dig into my skin. *They're eating each other.* Chains attach from the wolves' skinny bodies to the walls as they look up, with sleep encasing their bloodshot eyes, towards our quivering frames.

"What-" Jay gags as he opens his mouth but slams it shut as the scent of decay seeps into his nostrils.

"It makes it hard to kill things that look like us, you see," Dean says, prodding the head of a wolf carcass as ants scurry out of its white eyes. "It's just a few toxins injected into their bodies, nothing too big."

Dean shakes a small flask as she flashes us a light smile; the same purple formula of the Beast Tamer's on stage.

"But for a simple flower to render all werewolves to this state, Wolfsbane really doesn't fail to surprise me." she turns to Jay and pats his arm gently. "You can understand, right? It's nothing personal."

Dean's large arm drapes around my shoulder, and she slips the flask into her pocket.

"I knew I could count on you." she whispers to me, her hot breath scratching against my ears.

My teeth grit as I turn to Jay. His eyes are agape and intently trained on the repulsive sight. My face scrunches. *Why act now!?*

Dean drops the black collar into my hands, and the anticipation emitting from her makes it hard to breathe. I swallow the saliva building up in my throat and drop the white shawl to the floor. Cold rushes to my toes, and my sandals slide across the ground as my heart quivers in my chest. *I'm doing this for Daniel.*

My body smashes against Jay as I shove his head into the grey dirt. Weapons spill out of his bag as he fumbles for the Wolfsbane spray, directing it at me with an ugly growl. My nails thrust into his skin as I lash the can out of his grip, and blood trails down my fingertips - into my palm.

"Don't think I'll let you get away this easy, dipshit!" Jay screams, digging his fangs into my nape as he scratches against my chest.

I wince, clipping the black collar onto his neck, and ripping his grip off me. He dashes after my fleeing frame, bloodied hands scraping the floor as he faceplants into the earth. Electric shocks strike his body as suffocating cries leave his throat.

"You!" he gasps in-between breaths as foam bubbles at the corners of his mouth. "You knew from the start!"

My head sinks to the floor as I hold my bleeding wounds. The guilt, the pain, the disgust, I can't tell which one hurts the most.

"Acting like you don't know jack-shit about this place!"

That's not it. My eyes narrow as I glimpse at Jay's crawling physique.

"You know everything – that the humans are eating us, that I'm an Alpha, and that the Beast Tamers want me! So, you brought your damn owner to get to me first, huh!?"

I turn away from the rage gurgling within Jay's eyes. The longer I look, the deeper a pool of guilt I'll fall in.

"It would be quite the problem if he didn't," Dean says, holding down the button connected to Jay's collar. "Now, now, it's not like you're eager to become someone else's Blood Whore, right, Jay?"

Jay's fingers burst with blood as he scrapes at the ash earth. Sparks of electricity erupt within his system, and his eyes lie bloodshot as he snarls at my frame. Drool plops onto the soiled dirt as his body convulses from the pain. *He trusted me, and I broke that.* My fists clench as my heart aches and wounds continue to bleed. *Will you ever forgive me?* But those black eyes surging a thunderous storm only scream 'HATE' as they stab into me. Jay's form wriggles at my feet, panting for gasps of air and clawing at the dirt as I tower over him. As my eyes trace his tragic figure cursing my name, it's then I realise - the vile and horrible place I'd step foot in, The Butcher's Quarters, is what I've become.

WOLFSBANE

Waves of nausea engulf my body as the aroma of cooked meat clings to my throat. Werewolves wolf down their hard-sought meals, as the crunching of bones and smacking lips indicate their return from battle. Every open-mouthed chew roars fiercer than the surging storm brewing outside as the torn scent of rabbit flesh stings my nostrils, triggering the bumps against my tongue and the flips spiralling in my stomach. Red sauce drips from the werewolves' chins, and slabs of red meat shove into their mouths as they relish in the salty essence spilling into their gums. Bile burns at my throat, and my hand presses against my lips. A groan escapes my system as I sink deeper into the softness of the couch's cushions, bothered by the harsh yells rupturing my ears.

Behind the counter, Caretakers - chief of serving the foulest poultry dishes - reprimand mischievous werewolves stealing from their stock. Shoes squeak along the boarded floors as the wolves scramble away from the humans, basking in the thrill of mania. Chuckles escape from their systems, as their jobs, roommates, and relationships, are the least of their worries in this thriving moment.

My head tilts as a drink clatters from the vending machine. Nathan shakes a can of chicken blood with a large grin slapping across his face as he throws its chilled contents into my lap.

"Look who it is, Mr. Depresso!" he jeers, plopping himself into the comfiness of my couch. "Ever thought that a smile might just brighten up that face of yours?"

"Nathan." I sigh as my weary eyes barely take in his shaved head and muscular frame beside me, "I smuggled a child and destroyed his future for my benefit." I cradle the can in my palms as the cold liquid drenches my black jeans. It stands upright against the floor as my knuckles rub along my temple. "I couldn't be more... ecstatic."

Nathan smirks as he grabs the beverage and pops it open. Crimson dribbles down his neck as he engulfs its contents, and gulps protrude from his throat. My eyes narrow as I turn away.

"Then at least look it," he says, removing the can from his lips with a relieved sigh, "your depression's contagious, you know?"

"Please, turn back time. I'd love to consider it."

Nathan wipes the excess blood from his neck as he rests his elbow against the couch's rim.

"But didn't Jay go in voluntarily?" he asks, lifting his drink, "What would turning back time do?"

An exasperated sigh leaves my lips as I lean my head onto the cushion's edge.

"Word sure travels fast," I say, extending my branched limbs to give Nathan little space.

"Nah, you just attract attention way too quickly." he teases, kicking my legs with an enormous grin glued onto his face, "New-comer and all."

A glare stabs through Nathan's thick skull as I face his grinning physique.

"Is making fun of me your new hobby?" I ask, a frown crossing my features.

"Is it working?"

"No. Seeing your face for too long already gives me a headache." I state, shoving his legs onto the floor as I attain the room he'd taken from me.

"Unlike you, my daughter loves this gaudy face of mine," he snickers, stroking his goatee.

"Shave, you're probably growing lice in that beard. You won't be impressing anyone."

"And you think I'm trying to impress you?" Nathan scoffs as he wiggles his locket in his calloused hands. Its copper casing flicks open, and he stares at the scratched locket as if it's a hard-earned rhinestone. "Sorry to break it to you, but this dad is in love with his little girl." His voice cracks as the softness of his tone destroys the scarred, grizzly physique he upholds. As a young girl with bushy, black locks grins enthusiastically at him from the charm, as she puts her hand in the form of a peace sign. *Analisa, Nathan's daughter.* The stories he tells about her are incessant as if she's there, standing by his side and holding his hand. "I at least want her to remember my face the next time she sees me."

If that time ever comes. My head lowers as I stare at the polished tiles. How long has it been since we've worked here and never once gone to The Outside? As if just seeing it is an everlasting, senseless dream blown away by reality. Nathan's temple scrunches as if he's thinking the same, and he sighs.

"But my job with you comes first," he says, shutting the pendant, "and I'm sure you're 'ecstatic.'"

His grin widens as he stresses every letter, and I roll my eyes.

"What's the job?" I ask, tilting my head to Nathan as he throws his can away.

"A runaway Omega." he states, crushing the aluminium with his bare hands before dropping it into the trash, "The Butcher tried playing a little game with them, you see. But as usual, it didn't end well, and in order to hide their shame, they've given us – dogs of labour – the tiniest, minuscule piece of information they can muster."

My hand props against my chin as I raise my brow, "Which is?"

"A female with the number '237' on her stomach."

I lean forward as I wait for him to continue, "That's it?"

"What, you were expecting more?"

No, but- damn.

"That's vague."

"I know, right? I mean, what can we say? It's an embarrassment for the Butcher." Nathan shrugs as he strolls towards the outside of the cafeteria, and I follow in tow. "Just shows that too much entertainment is costly."

I grunt. *So, werewolves are merely child's play?*

The cafeteria's round tables jab us in the sides as orange lights illuminate our figures and cloak us in ginger skin. A cool breeze flushes onto our faces as we step out, and I jerk back as a small, thick-coated body rams into me.

Jay sneers at me with a scrunched face as he sucks his teeth and heads into the cafeteria. I want to call out to him, grab him by the shoulders, speak my mind, but my mouth opens towards his frame, and not a single sound leaves my throat. I bite my lip and close my eyes. *Because what can I even say? Sorry for destroying your life? What kind of shit apology is that?* I devoted myself to not involving him and look what I've done. It's an inevitable fate. No matter the excuses, nothing will erase the sin I've committed of turning his life into a torturous hell. My eyes train on his silhouette disappearing in the blinding, bronze light, and I groan. *If only he wasn't an Alpha.*

"Think you can get back to your room safely?" Nathan jokes, slapping my back.

"I doubt it."

Guilt eats at my brain. *I had to do it - there was no other choice. Not for me, but for someone else, it's inevitable…*

"Just giving you a heads up, I won't help you. It's your problem." Nathan retorts, smirking at me.

"Your definition of 'friends' is pointless," I grunt, jabbing him in the side as we head to the lobby.

"Shame I'm the only one you got, huh? You need to work a little bit more in that sector, bud."

"I'm glad you know how far your 'usefulness' goes," I say, heaving a sigh as my body stills.

A figure, drenched underneath the droplets of pouring rain, stands in the rectangular doorframe leading to my secret spot. Within the scent of wet dirt and muddied clothes, it looks at me with a distressed expression on its face, as if it's seeking my help, ushering me to enter its grasp.

"Hey…Gabriel."

I flinch. It's mouthing my name, and even though we're far apart, I can sense the once calming, mellow voice that lulled me to sleep.

"Do you know her?" Nathan asks, staring at the miniature physique trembling beneath our eyes.

Its eyes light up as they turn to me, a wavering smile touching upon its bone cheeks, and my heart blackens.

"No, I don't."

Its eyes widen as I tower over it.

"I don't know this sorry excuse of a werewolf," I affirm, staring at its shivering form similar to a rabbit shot by a huntsman.

"W-what do you mean, Gabriel?" *The stuttering – it's back.* "I-it's me… May-"

My eyes narrow as my hands ball into a fist.

"Don't lie to me, Kanya." I hiss, as a sound doesn't dare to leave its trembling lips.

My eyes glaze over its murky frame as a forced laugh escapes my throat, and I sneer at it. "Right, I don't know you."

Tears roll down its red cheeks as I turn away, and its dirty hands pull at my shirt.

"I'm sorry I lied to you! I didn't mean it; It's all just a misunderstanding; I promise Gabriel, give me another chance!" It pleads, wiping its snot and tears with wool sleeves turning from its light brown to dark in colour. "It was- It's because…I'm sorry, but I need you to…"

"I thought you said you didn't know her?" Nathan interjects, causing it to flinch.

Its form trembles in front of the door as wind lashes at its body from the inside. *No, I don't know this demon.* Tears fall from its eyes as the evil thing grips onto my shirt. *I don't know anyone like that.* I slap its hands away as it looks at me in disbelief.

"Hold on; I'll see her out," I say, ushering it forward as I rest my hand on its back.

"No, Gabriel, y-you can't, please!" It shrieks as it clings onto my body and its nails dig into my clothes.

You're still calling me by my name? My lip curls.

"Gabriel, I need you! Right now, I can't leave without you! If you're not here, I-"

Werewolves cluster to the noise with curiosity embedded in their systems as they observe the scene playing out in front of them. My brows furrow as heat flares within my chest, and I look at the trembling demon's tear-stained face with slitted eyes.

Pathetic. Still trying to tempt me with sweet words? Still trying to lure me into your traps of endless lies? To think I liked you once! To think I liked you once, and the feeling still lingers even now!

"You're walking on your own two feet, aren't you?" I blankly state as it shakes its head vigorously.

"Y-you don't understand."

"Then make it so I can."

Its hands blare a bright red as it releases its hold on my shirt and strokes my face.

"I can't!" It cries, tracing my eyelid. "Gabriel, I'm sorry, but you just have to trust me!"

Grime coats my body. Everywhere it touches, it lingers like an un-washable stain. It cries as if it's prey begging to be set free, touching the soft spots

112

of a predator about to devour it, but that's not it, is it? I'm just another pawn of your filthy game, *succubus*.

"All that time we spent together; those had been the best three months of my life." It sniffles, burrowing its body against mine. "I really, really don't want it to end like this, Gabriel."

Then where did you go?

"I can't be the only one who enjoyed our time together, right?"

Maybe you were.

"It wasn't just me, you also... you also like me too, don't you?"

My jaw clenches as it slides my hand around its neck and peers at me with those glass eyes. *Damn it. Damn it! Those days run through my head like a VHS recorder; you think I want them to end? Of course, I like you-* My heart falls. The patter of rain is like bodies slapping against the ground. The cold air clasps me in its grasp as my silver eyes stare at those trembling hues. Who's the prey, now?

"Gabe." Nathan interrupts, laying a hand on my shoulder. His brows furrow as he looks at the growing numbers of werewolves, and he gives me a stern look: 'Don't let it interfere with your work.'

"I don't." I declare as its small eyes widen with fear.

"I-I Gabriel, I'm sorry I lied to you. But today... It has to be today!" It begs, clinging to my physique. Its frame leans into mine as it yanks my collar desperately.

My nails dig into its knuckles as I yank off its grip. "Think you're the only one with circumstances!? Think you're the only one trying to live for themselves, to survive!? To fight everyday with others on your mind just to get you through the day!?" I shout, shoving its body to the floor.

"I-" It stutters in a daze as it stares at the white tiles.

"Get out," I say as I turn away from it. "Get out. You're interfering with my work!"

A stream falls down its dirty skin as its body shrinks and transforms into the milky, grey wolf I once loved.

"Thinking we had a connection, falling in love with you, all that time we spent together, Gabriel… was I really the only one?" It chokes in-between tears as it leaves its clothes behind and scampers on four legs out of the door.

You weren't. But when its physique disappears my stomach drops, and every inch of my body screams at my legs to move. *Go after her. You can fix this misunderstanding; just talk to her. Just speak to her!* My body sinks to the floor as I wrap my arms around my head. *What if she won't tell me the truth? What if it's another lie? What then?* Strangled groans burrow into my rolled sleeves as I bite my lip. *Everything is pissing me off. Why can I do anything but make things right?* Though, the one begging me to chase after her, is it my wolf nature or my human consciousness talking? My nails dig into my fingers as they tremble. *What do I want?*

Nathan slings an arm over my shoulder as his face beams with his signature grin.

"To think this scrawny boy could have lovers behind my back, since when were you such a play-"

"Cover me," I say, removing Nathan's grip and dashing into the downpour.

Rain pricks at my skin like needles as the icy wind slaps across my face. Trees crane in the tumultuous storm as my sandals squelch in the puddles of wet snow. *Maya, where are you?* Her scent dissipates in the daggers of cold rain as the road ahead is a dark abyss of lashing rain whips. Honestly, it's luck that I've travelled this same route for all my life here — the ocean of Wolfsbane, the weed-covered staircase, the shrine of our ancestors. The whole route lies imprinted in my head, and as I reach the pond, I desire to do everything in my power to forget it.

As lying in a puddle of scarlet wolfsbane is Maya. However, she isn't breathing or annoying me with tear-filled eyes. Instead, her face is a blank canvas of scarlet strings leaving her lips. Her raven strands are tangled and soaked from the pelting rain, and her body is distorted on the flowers of death. I step back, my heart hammering against my chest. The mannequin peers at me, stabbing into my soul with wide, black eyes as it encrypts a spine-chilling message:

Why didn't you come sooner?

THE WOLF IN SHEEP'S CLOTHING

Water gushes into my sandals as I drop into the wet soil. Wind gnaws at my soles, enshrouding my toes in pools of black mud as frostbite engulfs my body and sinks me deeper into the cold earth. My fingers tremble as I place a cold hand on Maya's neck. Frosty droplets roll down my cheeks and dots her pale face as it dribbles down my chin. *She isn't breathing.*

Branched limbs crackle in the atmosphere as the sky's scream summons the spectral glow shrouding Maya's body. Red lines extend from her forearms to her tangled fur, as clumps of dead flesh lie impaled by black talons. Purple bruises, from a Butcher's whip, run down her ankles to her pale toes as needle marks decorate her pale neck.

The silken fabric runs along my fingertips as I roll up her bodysuit. Tug after tug, my eyes widen as the numbers '237' drill a hole into my skull beneath the ink material. *Why didn't I realise sooner? But those bruises didn't exist the times we met, so how could I have known?* A shiver runs down my spine as the yellow tag, stapled on her abdomen, blares against my eyes.

It was the moment she disappeared, after she confessed to me, and I'd rejected her, these scars must've become visible. *Would things be different If I'd chosen differently? If I'd accepted, if I'd been with her. Wouldn't I have been able to save her?*

Though, why would I? I said so myself; It's fate, isn't it? My fingers stab into the clay soil as I pick up her motionless body.

"Shut up," I murmur. *I have Daniel. I know, but-*

Her head sways from side to side as I jog underneath the rumbling skies with the pelting rain smacking against my dark cheeks. *I could've saved them both.*

"Maya." I strain, as my hot breath flushes against Maya's frozen face. Icicles scratch the back of my throat as I swallow the chilled air streaming up my nose. Though, no matter how long I wait for a response, the howling winds and crumbling skies will be the only entities to meet my empty pleas. As the woman, identified as Kanya Vigolfr, stares listlessly at me, with dead, jet-black eyes as she lies motionless in my quivering arms.

"Stay away from her," Oliver warns with an eery grin lifting her pale cheeks.

My foot taps against the floor as my arms fold against my chest, "And why should I listen to you?"

"To think you're keen on messing with a Butcher's property," she teases, putting a pen to her lips as a pout distorts her sly demeanour, "you are more masochistic than I thought; would you like another lesson?"

Goosebumps crawl against my skin as ill-lit, blue hues peer at my shuffling physique. My head turns towards the door as an eery chuckle escapes Oliver's throat.

"Planning to listen?" she asks with a sardonic smile smacking across her face.

"Talk," I order, clutching the doorknob tightly in my grip as I eye her smirking frame.

"Gabriel." Oliver starts, curling the blackbird feathers clipped to her ears, "Have you ever seen an Omega within the dorms?"

"Quit beating around the bush and get to the point." I growl, a huff leaving my nose.

Oliver shifts to twirl her brown pen in her twig hands, and stares at me questionably as if the words are tangled upon her tongue. A sigh leaves her lips as she looks at me disdainfully. "The girl you're chasing is Blood Type O, an Omega."

What? My eyes shudder as they lock onto Oliver's blue pupils.

"Are you aware? Every Omega that enters the institute is immediately sold to the Butchers." Oliver says, tapping the pen rhythmically against her cheek. "I'm sure you've seen enough of the Butchers' works during your little expedition to know what they're capable of, right?"

If it weren't for you, I-

Oliver gestures to the black collar around my neck and puts a finger to her lips as she squints. *'You met me first.'* is what she'll say next.

I huff as I press my back against the wall.

"Where?" I ask, as a faint smile touches Oliver's lips.

"Their dead bodies are sold to Beast Tamers as 'light meals.' The infinite amount of power humans have to control us; you know where it comes from now, don't you?"

"But type O is-"

"The weakest and lowest wolf type," Oliver interjects, softly giggling at my scowling face, "As Beta, we're the most common werewolf type. Yet our strengths differ greatly, isn't that frustrating?

122

The arena we fight in weekly - Lacuna Dome. Its sole purpose is to train us, make us stronger, for the humans to preserve their meat supply, and last of all, to gain 'strength.' This 'work system' for us werewolves is simply a slaughterhouse. Think about it Gabriel, what do you think will happen if humans got their hands on the strongest blood type, Alpha?"

My eyes widen as my heart drops to my stomach. Oliver takes a step towards me as she senses my hesitation. The doorknob twists in my sweaty palms as I lean further into the grey wall with Oliver's eyes locking onto mine.

"They become a Beast Tamer..." I mutter in disbelief as Oliver's footsteps pound in my ears and she hums in agreement. "So, you're telling me I met with a ghost?"

Oliver stops in place with a puzzled expression crossing her features. "Not at all. Omegas can be given a chance to survive."

"They can?" I ask as a bead of sweat falls from my temple.

Oliver tilts her head and nods as she puts a hand to her chin. "By having their number picked from a roulette, similar to the ones we have for battle, they can live. However, the number chosen is forced to have pups with a strong male."

"What-"

"Do you know why no werewolves have been recorded to be from Outside, Gabriel?" Oliver asks, her feather earrings clinking against her bleached skin, "It's because we're born here."

"Kanya," I mumble, the realisation dawning upon me.

"Do you think it's coincidental?" Oliver asks, with a grin tugging her cheeks as she edges closer towards me. "That girl's number was picked, but she seems to have made a bit of a mistake."

A stern look wipes my face as Oliver clasps her hand around mine, "How?"

The doorknob squeaks in her tight grip as cold sweat swivels down my temple once she places her free hand beside my head.

"Top Dogs are known to be Alphas," she whispers lowly as her hot breath fans my neck. "Gabriel, you're a Beta, only known to be Top Dog in Bronze Rank because you have the strength to match an Alpha. Whether it made you lucky or unfortunate is your choice."

Sinister giggles emerge from Oliver's mouth as she digs her pen into my collar bone. My face twists in discomfort as squiggles appear on my coal skin.

"But you see, chosen Omegas have a time limit to mate," she says, staring up at me with wide eyes as she continues to draw.

"And if she doesn't?" I barely choke out as my sweat attempts to wash the marker passing on my skin like mud.

Oliver lifts her pen to reveal the amateurish drawing of a skull as she smiles with wide eyes. Her index finger points to her head, raising her thumb to the ceiling, as her face pales against her bright grin like a ghost's.

"She dies," Oliver finalizes, meeting my shivering frame, "She dies."

Blood trickles from my nails as I claw the wet dirt. Rocks pierce my palms with every handful, scraping my skin and searing new wounds as I scrabble at the overflowing clumps of mud.

"It was bound to happen; nothing I could've done would've made anything change, I-" My eyes train on the motionless girl lying in front of me as if my murmurs will suddenly resurrect her from the dead.

Soil rolls back into the holes I'd dug up as water gushes from the sky. Yet, I don't stop, I keep digging – till my hands ache, till my senses numb, till I can no longer move, or feel no more, just like…her.

"Gabe?"

Nathan towers over me with wide eyes as the sky's lights reveal his blotched face contorting in concern. The yapping of wolves and yells of humans emerge from behind him as he stares quizzically at my dirt-soaked figure. Blinding, white lights illuminate my frame, and I dash to Maya's body as I cradle it with tarnished hands.

"Nathan, can't you just...let this one slide?" I beg, pressing my nose into the earthy scent immersing from Maya's soft, black strands.

"Gabe, drop it!" Nathan orders, his eyes brewing a storm as he spits at my soaking frame. "Drop it before you regret it!"

"I can't," I murmur, caressing her damp fur in my tattered hands, "I can't."

"What's gotten into you, man!? Drop it!"

"I-"

Nathan yanks Maya's body from my loose grip as he slams me to the floor. My fangs bare at Nathan's beastly frame as Maya's pale face gets dirty from the black snow. Beastly claws seep into my neck, and Nathan's hoarse growl ascends to his throat. "Gabe. Drop it!"

I struggle underneath his grip as blood trickles down my collarbone. Werewolves and Beast Tamers approach the scene with flaring lights as they gape at our scrimmage. My eyes swallow

Maya's open-eyed frame beside me, the small pores decorating her face, the light birthmark inked below her bottom lip, her long, sparse, black eyelashes, everything. A blue tarp falls on her face, and the humans drag her body in the freezing rain. *No, don't take her! Leave her!* My claws stab into Nathan's shoulders as I plunge him into the wet earth. A groan escapes his system as I crawl to Maya's body. *You can't-*

Serpentine eyes snap at my dripping ones as they glower at me. My body sinks to the floor as Deianira D. Lobos stamps her heel onto the back of my hand.

The scraping of Kanya's dragging body resonates in my ears. *I want to scream. I want her back. I want her alive.* My lungs ache as tears roll down my cheeks. Nathan slams my face into the filthy snow as my dirt-filled eyes lock on Maya's every move. *It's my fault; I shouldn't have blamed you.* My palms ache for her touch, her soft smile, the words that make my heart continuously flutter. Yet, the more the seconds pass, and the tinier her silhouette becomes, the more the tears blur my vision. Her hand isn't going to reach out to me; I won't hear her voice anymore; I can't smell her sweet scent once more. She isn't coming back, because I didn't save her; I never did.

Maya is dead, and nothing can change that.

9
BAIT

he cold cement penetrates my back as I lie motionless on the concrete. Sun filters through the cracks of dilapidated bricks and onto my eyelids as the energy to turn away from the blinding rays remains non-existent. Sweat and blood washes over my nose as Maya's dead body drills into my mind and breaks my heart once more. The one I loved is Maya, but the stranger I killed is Kanya. A person I never knew, hidden behind the mask of an alias. *If she came out as the Omega, Kanya, instead of the Beta, Maya, would that day never have come?*

Chains clatter as the cage swings to and fro, hauling my body to the surface. My face scrunches the closer I get to the arena as the crowd's cheers and slurs penetrate my ears. Yet, the last thing I want is to go out there, emit from my secluded zone, and immerse into the place shrouded in light - Lacuna Dome.

The cage clanks, jolting my body upright, like thunder booming from yesterday's crumbling skies as the gates of the cage swiftly unlock. Wet sand sifts through the gaps of my toes as the blinding sun soaks my body in a godly ray. As I force myself across the grounds, ear-splitting screams from the sea of worn wolf furs ricochet off the yellow, stone walls, smeared in paw prints and blood-written words, as I stand at the edge of the battlefield.

"Ladies and Gentlemen, it's the moment we've all been waiting for, The Hunt!" The commentator cries, relishing in the crowd's applaud and cheer. Within a large, open veranda, atop the dying messages from previous contenders, the commentator makes a racket in his seat. "Today, we bring you, Gabriel Louvell, once Top Dog in Bronze Rank, and his successor, Jay Vigolfr as his opponent!"

My eyes widen towards Jay's scowling figure, beyond the stretches of wet sand, as he pierces a gaping hole through my skull. *Jay?* A sharp growl transcends from his throat as I choke on my saliva, thanks to gaping at him for too long. *This is nothing – it's just a race to take down the bait.* Yet, no matter how much I try to convince myself, uneasiness spills through my system like a broken dam, and my legs begin to give way as the betrayal of Jay's trust floods through my mind.

Grains of sand scatter into the air as the rock door, at the opposite end of the arena, shudders as it opens. Shadows overcast a large creature bellowing within as it steps onto the battlefield, making the earth quiver with its weight. Stone cracks underneath its hooves, silencing the wind as its dusky brown eyes cover the arena with its menacing aura.

"May I present to you the Hylaian moose! A two-metre giant that will be the lure of today's hunting contest!" The commentator screams, breaking his mic with its high gain staticity. "What excitement this is, for we don't know what'll happen to our two pups, as this fiend is no easy matter, weighing at 700 kilograms, a size that can kill a bear!"

I clench my fists as hair snakes itself around my body. Claws eject from my fingernails as my steel eyes burn gold once they set sights on the beast before me. The monster grunts, slamming its hooves against the pavement as it taunts me, chipping the stone with its mass.

"Are you ready?" The commentator questions as I position myself on the field.

Heartbeats brush against my ears as the crowd's blood churns frantically through their veins. Their breath tickles my skin as their bodies paint in a blue, yellowish hue, and my black lips splatter drool onto the arena's floor.

"Then, let the games begin!"

I spring at the horned beast, aching for my claws to delve into its thick flesh. My jaw stretches as my fangs reach for its bearded neck. As I dash, my view tilts, and I fall forward as the prey disappears in my sight. My hands tug on its tufts of fur, attempting to pull it down with me, but my grasp quickly loosens. Tingles prick through my body, and instead of the prey's scarlet decorating my fingernails, laps of blood excrete onto the thick sand as my head bashes into the concrete.

Bloodshot eyes glare at me as Jay's huge, furred fists remain connected with my face. Sand trickles between my eyelids, burning my eyes, as tears fall from my bloodied nose onto the arena's floor.

"Oh, this is? The games just started, but Jay is claiming the bait as his by attacking Gabriel upfront!" The commentator yells, jumping in his seat.

A huff echoes above me, and my eyes grow wide. A ball of sand scrunches in my palms as Jay's knuckles bleed from the contact of my cheekbones. Aggravated cries protrude from Jay's throat as I toss the handful of sand into his eyes, and a hoof, the size of my face, crashes beside me. *If I were a second late, my death would've flashed before my eyes.* Though, now's not the time to avert my attention. My eyes narrow towards Jay's enraged form and the large deer.

"Jay-!" I call out, reaching to his monstrous frame, but raging, black eyes and glittering, white fangs, desiring my blood, glower at me instead.

"Don't *say* my name." he demands, a snarl escalating his throat as he sends chill after chill spiralling into my stomach.

134

I glimpse at the moose flaring its nostrils and shaking its antlers as I turn to Jay. My heart leaps in my chest as I dash to the edges of the arena with Jay pacing behind me without a second thought. His lips open, throwing imperceptible words at my figure, and as I run, the more haggard he appears.

"Why...why was your scent on her body?" he mumbles as my running gradually slows down.

"What-"

Air thrusts out of my lungs as I knock to the ground with a crushing weight against my ribs. A cracked and miserable growl follows after, as Jay's stained, white daggers snap at my face with spit splattering onto my dark mane.

"WHY WAS IT YOU WHO FOUND KANYA INSTEAD!?" Jay screams as his eyes fill with a turbulent matter of rage.

His paws tighten around my throat as my fur dampens with spit and sweat. So many questions roll through my mind, but with so few answers. He belongs to Dean, so he saw Kanya's body, but why would this arrogant, ignorant, son of a bitch, care for someone who's none other than an Omega!?

135

"What does it matter to you?" I spit as his calloused hands tremble along my raven mane.

"What does it matter to *me*?"

A laugh erupts from Jay's stomach as tears roll down his eyes and plop onto my nose. Such a dark and dreary laugh freezes me, even as he regains his composure and tightens his grip around my neck.

"The girl you killed was my sister." he calmly states, with a dark, sinister tone that makes my ears flatten and tail tuck between my legs.

Your sister?

I can't breathe. If I inhale, the thickness of Jay's bloodthirst and statement will kill me. *She has a brother, doesn't she?*

"Then, where were you?" I snap, suppressing my guilt as anger takes over, catalysing the rush of everything that has happened and hitting me all at once. "WHERE WERE YOU!?"

My claws dig into Jay's skin as crimson droplets drop onto my tongue. "If you're her brother, you would've protected her! And where were you!?"

"I was looking for her!" Jay finalizes, plummeting my body back into the sand. "And instead, she found you, her killer!"

The iciness from the phrase gives me frostbite.

"I didn't...I didn't kill her... I-"

My eyes fall to the floor as a growl erupts from Jay's chest and his fist slams me deeper into the stone.

"Then who did?"

With an electrocuting stare, Jay thrusts another fist against my skull.

"Say it to my face! Who did!?" he yells as blood pours out of my mouth, staining the golden molecules pressing against my back. "I don't give a shit what you do to me, but you crossed the damn line when you touched Kanya!"

Jay's claws seep into my flesh as my canines weakly pierce into his thickly, furred forearms. My head slams back into the concrete as he slaps my muzzle to the side, and blood oozes into the arena as the world starts to blur.

"How should I have known?" I mumble as tears cascade from my eyes.

"You should've!" Jay exclaims, blocking my airways as I profusely scratch at his wrists. "You should've... 'cuz ever since she came here, she's only tried to find you!"

His voice is hoarse as the water from his throat dries out completely. Snot and tears drip from his frame and onto my fur coat as I struggle in his hold. "She kept on yapping and yapping about that 'Top Dog' in Bronze Rank. The damn name making my head hurt, and to think; it was my roommate."

My lungs ache, and my ears ring as the world sways before me.

"Are you seriously planning to kill me?" I manage to choke out. "Dean will-"

The grin touching Jay's lips is faint.

"You talkin' bout the people up there, enjoying this? I'm doing them a favour," he says coldly. "It doesn't matter who wins this shitty competition. They're going to have a tasty meal tonight, and you won't let them down, Gabriel."

Jay's claws imprint on my neck, rupturing my cells as they tear through my muscles and crack my bones. My fingers fall against the sand as his hands tighten even further. The deafening cheers become distant as the darkness slowly cascading my view feels like bliss. People are screaming, but it's due to the excitement. The commentator's booming voice isn't dominating the stadium anymore; it's peaceful. My lips quiver as I can no longer struggle. Even if I reflect on what I'm fighting for, Jay's hold on me doesn't waver. Strength saps away from my system – little by little – as I drop to the arena's brick floor, and the last thing I note once my head hits the sand is Deianira D. Lobos, staring at me from afar.

KARMA

Cold water splatters onto my skin as my hot breath fans against my face. My head pangs, drilling my nails into the wet soil as cold shivers run down my body. My system is screaming - from the unwashed pain, from the guilt, from the dark, red wounds and large bruises scattered across my frame – lunging me back into reality. I grunt as I heel over, shaky breaths leaving my quivering lips. I attempt to close my eyes, immerse in the silence as the coolness of the underground and the darkness of near-death – slightly, but surely - washes my system like ecstasy, but it's to no use. My body heaves as I plummet into the clay earth and sharp coughs crush my throat.

A downpour of icy droplets splashes onto my frame, and its icy suffocation tightens against my chest. I groan as I grab a handful of dirt. The water's burning through my pores and gnawing at my skin – *I can't breathe.* With glazed eyes, I whimper towards Dean's smirking silhouette, behind black bars, as she orders another bucket.

"If I knew you were so eager to die in your sleep, I wouldn't have wasted my time getting involved in the first place," she says, dumping the third bucket onto my quivering physique. "But now that you're awake, I guess it's for the best."

A clang sounds within the cell as the steel basin drops to the floor.

Dean smiles wickedly as she taps her red, needle-like nails on her round face, and crosses her wide legs on a chair positioned outside the cell. Behind her, a shelf with multiple toxins gleams in my vision as she sneers at me, "Don't you have something to say to me?"

My blue lips tremble as I glare at her righteous frame. Air leaves my lungs, and I hack with an overwhelming shock shattering my system. I groan as drool splatters onto the wet earth and mucus streams from my nose.

"Right, I forgot. Manners don't simply appear if they didn't exist in the first place." Dean states, twisting her head away from my nauseous physique.

Droplets of sewage water drip from the ceiling and onto my nose as pants erupt from my chest while I claw the ground for dear life.

"W-why." I gasp, swallowing profusely, as my body shudders from the coughs leaving my lips.

Dean anchors her wolf coat on the wooden chair before directing her attention towards me.

"Gabriel, listen," she says lowly, her seaweed-green hues penetrating my figure. "Between contractor and hirer, I'd like there to be no secrets between us. So, answer me, why did you try to hide the body?"

I scoff, or so I thought I did, as a hack escalates my throat, and the cold fluid infiltrates my lungs. *Of course, this woman will spare me with the mere thought of punishing me for my past mistakes. I was stupid to think even for a second; she needs me...alive.*

"Has it inconvenienced you?" I question, a slight smirk tugging at my lips as I eye her pompous frame.

"A little bit." she confesses, picking at her nails, "If you died out there, it wouldn't be me, but the Omega's owner who would've gotten their hands on you."

My smile instantly drops. *They were watching. The Butchers, the people who killed Kanya – they were watching.* Fury and anxiety pulses through my veins. The massacre won't stop at Kanya; any wolf that dies will be-

"And after all that time I raised you, you can't expect me to simply let you go. I can't possibly do that." she coos as if she's a mother cradling her new-born child.

"And what if I wanted to stay-"

"When did your opinion matter?"

The cage bars shudder as Dean's palm slams against them.

"Gabriel, are you so slow to not realise your life belongs to me? As long as you look after that boy, your identity will stay as The Human's Watchdog for as long as you live. Because no matter what you do, you're afraid to leave him, aren't you?"

I scramble to the steel bars of the cage as my hands tremble. The icy metal bears into my nose as I gape at Dean's large figure.

"How-" I mutter, and Dean's eyes lighten with a smile.

"You don't think we keep werewolves inside here without any information, do you?" she says darkly, gesturing for slabs of shaved, red meat to be brought into the room.

Drool drips from the roof of my mouth as the waft of cow's meat settles upon my tongue once the werewolves descend the stone staircase. My stomach gurgles as the pleasant aroma weighs against my palette, and I lick my lips.

"Then again, it's your choice." Dean finishes, opening the cell and setting the meal onto the wet dirt.

My stomach twists as it bellows in frustration. Balls of saliva drop onto the earth, and my teeth ache for the tear of soft flesh and its juicy oils dissolving into my gums. I glance up at Dean's lingering presence within the cell, and I swallow deeply.

"It's not good to force yourself," Dean says, walking out of the confinement with a sinister smile.

My hand dives for the helping as the click of the cell penetrates my ears. I ram the meat into my mouth, ripping its tender tissues as its juices slide down my tongue, closing my wounds. *This is bliss.* It's been days since I've eaten a meal, and the impact of meat after a battle is like no other. Regeneration takes stamina and energy. The more I wound myself, the bottomless my stomach becomes. If I'm not careful, my body will eat itself to heal, and it'll lead to malnutrition or death; a curse bestowed upon every werewolf. I continue to grind the large chunks of meat as my stomach rumbles joyfully. The saltiness of the meat weighs into my cheeks as I fill it to the brim and lick my blood-coated lips. My hand lunges for the next slab till my fingers freeze, and my chewing comes to a stop. *Punishment, that's what it is, right?*

My pupils linger on Dean's wide grin, and tears line my eyes as my mouth begins to rot. My knuckle crushes the plate as the once pleasant aroma turns repulsive and foul as it cascades from my lips. A strangled grunt leaves my system as a ball of meat jams my throat. Incoherent words fall of my tongue as I scrape at the dirt, and salty droplets spill from my eyes.

"What's wrong? Is it not to your liking?" Dean asks innocently with a cackle following after.

My jaw grits as my eyes burn a piercing yellow. That pungent, rotten, fish odour digging into my nostrils, *why hadn't I noticed sooner!? This damn dish wrapped in such a heavy scent of werewolf!?*

"I definitely thought it might be since you two were so close…" Dean hums, meeting my agape yellow hues, "Was I wrong?"

My body shivers as filth accumulates upon my tongue and my system roars to regurgitate.

"What do you mean?" I mutter.

"Oh, were the additives too strong? Or maybe you were just too hungry to notice? Your dear Omega, that Butcher gladly gave it away for free. A nuisance, he called it, not even worth his time," she says coolly with a sly grin hiding beneath her unfazed façade.

My nails scratch the back of my throat as slops of half-digested meat splatter against the ground. *Why? Why wasn't it all coming up?* Tears gush down my cheeks as I continue to retch, slamming my head into the soaked earth. Rocks pierce my temple and scrape my gums, as I bite into the soil and witness the sediment grains falling from my lips. My jaw slams shut as it pierces my tongue between my teeth, and my lips start to decay. I beat my head into the ground with snot dribbling from my nose and blood smearing onto the surface.

"It's Kanya…" I cry, the taste of blood and meat lingering upon my tongue. "It was Kanya…"

"After all the hard work you did to hide her body. It's a shame she's right in front of you, isn't it?" Dean snickers.

I gag as my guts twist, and my puke saturates the brown soil. I'm unknown, neither human nor werewolf - the fact of eating my own kind roaring through my body. My head slams against the soil as I scream against it. My tongue burns – from the wounds, from the meat, from the enraging desire to rip it out. I slump against the soil in a bath of my blood and vomit as soft cries leave my throat.

"I'm looking forward to seeing you at work tomorrow." Dean chuckles as she exits the vicinity.

I stare blankly at Dean's broad figure, leaving through the steel bars enclosing me, and surrender underneath the orange light flickering against my eyelids. The smell of acid penetrates my nostrils as I pass a vomit-soaked hand through my hair. Tears burn my cheeks as I cuddle my knees, and a soft laugh escapes my lips. *I should've died yesterday.*

HOWLS OF MISFORTUNE

Pebbles crack against the pavement as my bare feet trample over blunt stones. Between the large spaces of concrete, the wind whistles and masks our footsteps as they resound through the open corridors. Oak banners curl from Dean's underground dungeon to her bright, pink bungalow as every heartbeat, every breath, every movement lies within earshot as we escalate the stairs of hell in an unbearable silence.

149

"How has it been?" I ask, breaking the awkward silence, "Was I missed?"

Nathan didn't bat an eyelid since accompanying me from my cell, and he continues to pay no attention to me as if walking with a traitor is a grave sin.

"Sorry man, but I gotta admit." he starts, scratching his shaved head, "A morning without your dry ass complaints is a good morning. You should go out more often."

What deems as his normal, sarcastic comments eats at me like the truth. *'I don't want anything to do with you anymore'* is what he inadvertently wants to say.

Pain bubbles in my chest. "Sorry to disappoint, but I already feel like I died once. I don't need to experience that again," I say, heeding his words.

Nathan grins, a sly grin I'd never imagine catching on his face, and my eyes unconsciously widen.

"You might not," he says lowly, his eyes glowing with contempt, "but if another had a chance, he'd bulldoze you to the ends of the earth till he was satisfied."

I stare at him dubiously; is he talking about himself? *Nathan, do you want to kill me?*

Nathan nudges me in Jay's direction as we enter Dean's quarters, and a sigh of relief escapes my lips. The scars Jay imprinted on me from Lacuna Dome continuously stung. The more I look at them, the more his distorted expression appears in my mind, and the closer of a resemblance I can see between him and his dead sister, Kanya.

"How'd you like the sound of that? Too accurate?" Nathan jests, pulling me to Dean filling a glass of wolf blood from the blood transfusion bottle.

"Now that I'm here, I finally realise the last person I wanted to see was you," I state blankly.

"Come on. Don't be like that," Nathan teases, jabbing me in the shoulder, "the truth hurts, pal. Want me to play matchmaker?"

So, you don't have to get rid of me, yourself?

"Don't even think about it." I snap, shoving Nathan aside to pick up a box of black collars, similar to ours, by Dean's side.

"Woah, woah," Nathan says, putting his hands up in defence. "Looks like Mr. Depresso is Mr. Aggresso, and you talk to me about girls?"

"Nathan…" I groan. Just having a conversation with him makes my head hurt.

"You had it rough, man. We get it, but you won't cheer up 'till *you* decide you want to be happy."

My teeth grit. *What do you know about what I've been through!? Don't talk as if you understand. If your loyalty is so much more important, you should just quit playing 'friends' with me and assist Dean like a true dog!* My hands clench as I turn to Nathan. *Especially if it gives you no benefit if I'm alive.*

"No," I finally manage to say, unclenching my hands, "your optimism is just too much for me."

Nathan sighs as he shakes his head. "At least I tried."

He leads me to a blank corridor of stone without a single spec of decoration inked against it - a part

152

of Dean's quarters I've never been through before. The further we walk, the gradual transition from a stone wall to glass arises, and the more the transparent, blue crystal glimmers as it's hit by the moonlight filtering through a tiny room's barred windows. Within the room, Dean stands poshly with a glass of blood atop her round belly as the werewolves, and I, enter under her command at once.

A room of despair, with torturous metal equipment dangling from the walls, and only one door at the back of the room. The bustling of lorries from the outside and the deeply scratched tiles. *How can I forget? I've been here before.*

My eyes dart to the box of collars I have in hand. *Three, five, six? No, there're only four.*

Sobs and growls emerge from the backdoor, as four werewolves with large wounds tattooed against their bodies and muzzles fastly tightened against their face file in. Dean lifts her hand once all the adolescent werewolves come in, and those owned by her scuffle to block off the entrance. I too, take my position at the far side of the slate door as the small werewolves in Bronze Rank shiver underneath Dean's gaze, and nostalgia rushes over me like a tidal wave.

'Don't touch them!' I'm begging to scream, but as much as my system aches at the sight of those trembling wolves beneath Dean's touch, this is my last chance to prove my loyalty to the Beast Tamer, Deianira, and I don't need to lose it. *It's all for Daniel.*

Yet, every flinch from the young werewolves makes my blood boil, shouting at me to do something, to move, to not watch, to save them! They are alone with nowhere to go, in a situation one can never resolve unless swearing one's loyalty to Dean. *What makes them any different from me?*

My nails dig into my palms as my breaths slowly calm down my wavering heart. Nathan's mahogany eyes are drilling into me – I can sense it. His skin's pressing against mine, ready to hold me down if I make one wrong move, but it's okay.

I've got it under control.

"Dad?" A young werewolf squeaks as she stares at me. A she-wolf with tear-filled eyes, and dark, thick, black curls, one would have great difficulty passing a comb through, faces me with large, glistening pupils, "Is that you?"

My brow rises as the young girl turns her head to the side - *she's not talking to me.* My head cranes to Nathan, trembling at the sight of this little girl. The man with the image of a bear is murmuring words I can't understand as he stares at her in fear.

"Annie?" Nathan finally mumbles questioningly, as if he isn't too sure whether or not he is in the midst of a dream.

Analisa? My eyes train on her smooth, brown skin and freckled cheeks. *But why?* Nathan scurries to Dean with trembling lips, turning blue the longer they quiver.

"There's got to be a mistake!" he says breathlessly, refusing to take in Analisa's shivering form, even for a moment, "She shouldn't be here!"

Dean stares at Nathan disapprovingly as he flinches underneath her gaze.

"A couple of werewolves wandering further than they should have and entering Beast Tamer territory. Is that *not* trespassing to you?" she asks as the coldness in her voice sends ice trailing down everyone's skins.

Nathan too, doesn't dare look directly at the Beast Tamer or prod her with another question as he sinks into the room's shadows with dejection written all over his face.

"Then, if not all of them, please just let my daughter go." Nathan whimpers, scratching the inside of his hands.

Are you insane? All these kids, beaten and bruised, you experienced the exact same treatment, and you choose now to be selfish because of one person!? My claws dig into my arm sleeves. *But then again... who am I to talk?*

Dean glances at Nathan's shivering frame as blood drips from his palms, and he bites down on his lips. Her electric hues dart from Analisa to Nathan; then, a smile graces her lips.

"Suppress him." she commands, and the werewolves restrain Nathan's bulky body as they weigh him into the ground.

"Please!" Nathan begs, struggling in the werewolves' grip. "Let her go, at least!"

Nathan's voice cracks as he slumps in the hold of Dean's werewolves with tears pricking his eyes.

"Dad!" Analisa screams, with skinny, tawny legs scuttling to her father's side and her leash trailing behind. Blood pours from her nose as her face smacks against the concrete once Dean's heel stamps on her leash.

Half-bitten fingernails scrape at the floor desperately, as Analisa whimpers for her dad with glossy eyes. Tufts of fur surface upon her skin, but it soon returns rough and dry as her stomach splats against the silver tiles, and Dean's foot presses into her lower back.

"ANNIE!" Nathan screams with growls rupturing his system as he struggles in the Werewolves' hold and the others racing to hold him down.

Analisa coughs as her back hits against the wall, and her hand weakly reaches towards Nathan's floundering figure. A weight falls into her chest as

Dean stomps on her torso and pulls on her leash, revelling in her choked gasps.

"No! Please, not her!" Nathan yells, with tears streaming down his brown, furred face and glimmering, amber eyes.

Analisa's painful groans echo within the room as the leash prints dark bruises along her neck. Foam bubbles along the rims of her mouth, as her chokes become faint and her eyes appear distant. Her half-lidded eyes close, and her body slumps against the floor as a shaky breath leaves her lips.

The box of collars spills to the floor, and blood drips onto my furred muzzle as my teeth sink into Dean's skin. The crunching of bones and muscles sounds in my ears as I chew further into her thick hand, ripping her tendons. A yell escapes Dean's croaky throat, and my head slams into the silver stone as she tries to shake me off. A whine bursts from my muzzle as I gaze hazily at the young werewolves, and a rumble erupts in my throat as Dean's blood drips from my lips.

"Go, Get out!" I scream, with crimson pouring from my ears and bloodshot eyes from the impact of Dean's throw.

"This place… isn't what you think it is!"

DEMISSION

"**D**oes this look like a circus to you?" Dean spits, slamming my head into the concrete as sweat drips from her temple. Her red-stricken eyes glare at her werewolves as her teeth grits. "I asked, does this look like a circus to you!?"

Strained swallows pass within the room as Dean's werewolves lie bewildered at my large, four-legged body chomping on their master's limb, and they answer in tow, "No ma'am."

"Then stop gawking like clueless mutts and restrain this damn cur!" she screams, weighing a kick into my stomach as I double over against the wall.

Shaky breaths leave my mouth as I paw towards the shivering adolescents.

"Get out," I say weakly as Dean's werewolves lurch to dig their fangs into my body. "Everything…Everything you've heard is a set of lies!"

Dean's glass shatters beside my head, and a yelp erupts from my throat. Heat fuels in my ears as a deafening ring penetrates my brain, and my eyes tremble at Dean's fuming figure.

"*Don't* say another word."

Shivers roll down my body as her words leave a trail of ice, shaving my brown skin. Fangs clutch my fur, and clawed hands tug at my muzzle as I lie dazed by Dean's words, but what do I have to lose?

My eyes meet Analisa's shaking ones as tears roll down her cheeks, then to Nathan's. Biting through the hands weighing on me, I scream. With the breaking of my throat and the leftover air swirling in my lungs, I scream with all my might.

"This isn't a protection zone; it's a slaughterhouse!" My claws dig into the werewolves' flesh as they struggle to hold me down. My body twists in their grip, bloodying my canines with their blood as I shove through their un-faltering strengths, "The Outside won't exist if you end up dead!"

Analisa's breath catches in her throat as she plays back my words.

"So, if you don't want it to be a mere fairy tale and want to live the life you hope to live, get the hell out of here!" I yell, nipping the young werewolves' legs as they run past.

Electric shocks strike through my system, and my once courageous, righteous speech ends up for nought; my mind's blank. Dean's fingers continuously slam onto the shock button as froth emerges from my black lips. Large hands grab at my convulsing body as they take the chance to hold me down once and for all. Jabs and stings erupt from all sides of my curled form, and I can't tell if it's from the unsheathed talons prodding at my figure or the electricity surging through my veins. I gasp harshly as the pain wrecks my body, and scarred, ecru, beige legs stop in front of me.

"Get out," I choke as every shock sends my body into a seizure. "Please… you're not safe here."

The young boy looks at me with a blank stare. His long, black locks drape his face in an aura of gloom before he turns on his heel to follow the other teenagers. *He must be the last one.* A relieved huff leaves my nose as I watch the adolescent boy's body fade into the distance—*the quietest one.* The boy had an unstained face, devoid of tears, but instead painted with countless bruises and scars, unlike the other werewolves.

A devastating cry scratches my throat as Dean slams her heel into my face. Blood pours out of my black nose, and my tongue lolls onto the chilled ground as I look up at my previous master with tear-filled eyes.

"You've said too much." she states, lifting her heel once again off the ground.

My eyelids shut tight as I await the pain to slither down my body. *I can't move.* Werewolves clutch at my fur from all sides, and all I can do is cry.

"Gabriel, are you testing my patience?" Dean asks, slamming her heel into my muzzle once more,

"How many chances do you think you have? I don't know about you, but I don't consider myself to be that generous."

Squirts of blood rise into the air as Dean pushes her heel into the front of my face and hits my front teeth. I can no longer smell the scarlet dripping from my nose anymore. I claw at the ground as I struggle to stand up, to avoid the immense catastrophe about to fall upon my feeble frame, but I'm held time and time and again by werewolves – Dean's werewolves and not my 'kin.' Tears roll down my eyes from the pain, from the shock, from the limited air I'm allowed to breathe, and I can't say a word.

"Though seeing all the chances I've given you, I might perceive myself to be a nice person." Dean sneers, revelling in my shrieks as she peels off my nose with her heel. "Since you're so eager to get in my way, being part of the Butchers' stock, you wanted so much, will be enough to suffice for your actions, don't you think?"

Dean lifts her leg to fish the cylindrical bottle of a purple formula within her pocket. Her blood smears onto her white, fur coat as she winces at the stabs of pain pulsing through her hand. Her electric eyes glare at my captive figure as she takes out a syringe and stabs it into the circular bottle.

"And Nathan," she says coldly, glaring at the half-transformed mocha werewolf. "I'm very sure you know, a few stray wolves running around this place won't be enough to keep them away from me. So, with this chance I'm giving you now, you won't disappoint me, will you?"

A snicker dresses her lips as she passes the full syringe to Nathan. "You're in charge."

Nathan stares wide-eyed at the formula, and gulps. His transformation reverts as he cradles the deathly substance with shaky hands and turns to me.

"Gabe, I'm sorry... I'm sorry, man, but I-" Nathan presses the syringe shakily against my raven coat as his voice sticks in his throat.

The cold metal pricks into my skin, and I want everything, everything in my power not to die here, to not succumb to this shitty drug. *Daniel needs me.* Tears pour down Nathan's face as he grips my mane, and my mouth moves before I have time to think.

"Does your daughter want this?" I question, eyeing his stilled hands. "Is this what she knew her dad to be? A murderer who kills his friends?"

"We aren't friends! We never were!" Nathan snaps, but no matter how flustered he is, no wolf is a fool to sense the hint of regret trembling in his voice. His nails rip apart my blood-ink fur as they dig into my skin, and a growl rumbles in my throat.

"You're right. Because my only friend was a father that protected his child, not his status! Is that how much you care for her, Nathan? Spending nights reminiscing about the times you were together. That heartened look you have in your eyes when you see that locket. Did you really want to see her again?"

"Shut the hell up!" Nathan shouts, tightly gripping my wounds, "You don't know anything!"

"Nathan," Dean says, nudging Nathan with her foot, "time is precious, don't think I like waiting."

"But will you ever get out to see her again?" I continue, enduring Nathan's sharp nails digging into my sable fur. "We're werewolves, Nathan - an oppressed species commanded by humans. As soon as we're born, we're predestined to become the humans' pets, but that's not all we are, right? We have a choice, just like your choice to end me now, and your choice to save Analisa."

A punch lands in my gut, and my system screams louder than before. Another hand pushes my head further into the concrete as they dig their nails into my nape.

"Give me that." Jay spits, yanking the syringe off Nathan. "I don't give a shit what you're on about, but talking bullshit seems to be your forte, don't it? If you like flapping that dead tongue of yours so much, I'll do you a favour and send you to hell quick enough."

My ears bend back as a cry arises from my throat, "No! Don't-"

It's too late.

A stabbing pain erupts through my body as my system shuts down. Sparks flare within me, heating my face as I break into a cold sweat. My guts are eating themselves, pulverizing each other as they fight an all-out war against this unknown substance flowing through my veins. Despite the layers of blood staining my teeth and lips, my throat is dry; I can't even swallow. My body's frozen in place. *What is this?* Stings penetrate me from all sides, as my ears continuously ring to the tremendous amount of noise surrounding me.

Make it stop.

Make it stop!

The werewolves pick up my limp body, but my sense of touch dulls, and all I see is Jay's glowering pupils cursing me and Nathan's stunned ones. I attempt to close my eyes, but barbed wire pierces my sclera, and eyelashes scrape my bottom eyelid like a grater. Black infiltrates my vision, and I want to rest; I'm eager to. I run in and out of consciousness – a continuous cycle. Waking up from the pain, sleeping because of the pain, waking up from the pain, sleeping… the painstaking cycle continues. Only momentarily, as I truly succumb to the poison wires tied against my eyes, a sense of peace washes over me. As a honey milk-scent and a tearful smile fills my view within the darkness. Maya, the one I know and love, is smiling that same teasing grin I can't bear to forget at me. I can't hear her, touch her, feel her, but I can see her, and that was enough. She's alive, and that's all that matters.

THE REAPER'S DESCENDANCE

ire blazes through my system as my skin scorches with fresh wounds refusing to heal. My fingernails drill into my skin, picking at lice nesting in my fur, as scarlet overlays my nails and highlights the frequent colour seen amidst the sea of corpses. Maggot ingested wolf bodies, and bright yellow tags litter the floor as crushed skulls jut out of the dirt, portraying a feast for famished insects lurking in the walls. *What an ending, in The Butcher's Quarters, among the*

Omegas and Strays. My cellmate is no less fortunate, as an oak, wolf coat with a slung open mouth ogles me with pale, orange eyes as they hang along the cracked cement. *It's only time, till I'm next.*

My hand swats at the flies buzzing in my ears as the nauseating odour of decay strengthens in the room. Spiderwebs lace my fingertips, clutching onto my skin, and a groan erupts from my system as falling dust drops onto my nose. *Damn it.* My watery eyes turn to the line of dead bodies behind the wooden beams, and my fist slams into the dust.

Coughs shake my body as jolts spark through my system, and harsh gasps tighten my lungs. Painful grunts leave my lips as bloodlines imprint upon the grey earth as I convulse. My teeth clamp onto the insides of my cheek as I suppress a scream. My voice bubbles from my throat, and a soft murmur escapes into the atmosphere as salty droplets seep into my fur. *I'm not turning back.* My body quivers as jabs penetrate all sides of my body in an attempt to convert to a human, but my body's not listening to me - *I can't turn back.*

White light burns my eyes, eating at my retina, as the click of a switch resonates off the cracked walls. The wooden stairs creak as it weighs from the weight of those descending it. Glistening eyes face the entrance; as for others, this could be a nourishing delight, but for me, a continuation of this nightmare.

Dust disperses into the air as Oliver strides into the room with a small boy by her side. A foxy smile adorns her face as she stops in front of me and twirls her keys along her long, half-gloved fingers.

"They could've brought a better reaper," I growl, biting my lip. Dust accumulates at the back of my throat, and it isn't easing the itchiness flaring upon my skin.

"Am I disappointing?" Oliver asks, cocking her head to the side.

"Very."

"But seeing Kanya truly would've sent you to the Underworld." she snickers, gazing at my thorned hairs and sharpened, yellow eyes. "Was that offensive?"

"Do what you came here for and leave!" I spit, my claws inching longer as the seconds pass.

"Honestly," Oliver sighs as she removes her sights on me and onto the furred decoration fixed upon the wall, "to think there'd be a day, a Watchdog of Deianira's pushes her this far. Are you hiding more lives?"

My brow furrows, "And what does that have to do with you?"

"It's not often I'm able to see someone as lunatic as you, that's all," she says, as a hoarse growl erupts from my throat.

"I think the same when pets like you lick the feet of their owners!"

"I wouldn't say that if I were you," Oliver states calmly, "You were lucky."

My pupils follow her gaze to the sheen, walnut coat. Amidst the scent of the dead, a familiar smell of wildflowers, slightly damp from the rain, emanates from its fur. The skin beneath is bright red as if the mane had been cut recently. I was sure, if my hand went through it, splotches of blood will overlay my palm.

"Nathan…?" I mumble, reaching for the oversized, brown coat with wide eyes.

His ginger eyes penetrate my skull, and his white pearls shine towards my figure. The longer I face his state, the more insignificant the word 'sorry' becomes. *Of course, Dean will never give up the chance to gain a coat as rare as his.*

My teeth grits as heat fuels against my face. "How did you know!?"

Oliver's eyes glaze over my flushed physique uninterestingly as she continues to play with her keys. "I don't think it's unnatural for a Butcher's dog to fetch leftovers."

You-

"You didn't tell me you were working for them," I state, running my eyes over Oliver's figure. She has never worn a black collar until today. *So, she can take it off freely whenever she pleases?* My eyes narrow as my hands ball into fists. *Different owner – different rules.*

"You never asked." Oliver retorts.

"And by Butcher's, you mean-"

"The human that killed Kanya is my owner."

My heart stops. The passage of blood flowing through my veins halts as those words leave her mouth. I meet Oliver's stoic expression with my distorted one. *Yet, you can say that so naturally, as if life means nothing to you.*

"You already knew what was above the wall," I mutter, her face not changing even for a second, "and that 'tiny' errand you wanted me to carry out was to send me to my death."

Silence fills the room as Oliver's eyes pierce into my soul. *I don't need an answer.*

My jaw clenches harder, and it takes the tiniest bits of sanity to refrain from tackling this woman to her death. "Not just that, you watched Nathan die, and you killed Kanya; why are you-!"

"My owner killed her." Oliver states. "And do you think it makes a difference if one or two wolves die in this vicinity? We live in a place full of murderers, and *you* are no different."

My bear paws drill into the ground as I crawl towards the witch with fangs eager to snap her neck.

"At least I TRIED to make a difference. I refused to let my kind suffer, and I kept my pride as a wolf!" I yell, my chest suffocating my heart as I finish my sentence.

"And? What was the results of that?"

My body drops to the floor as Oliver kicks me into the earth. The bone-filled dirt rubs against my flared skin as I writhe in a curled ball and curse Oliver's name. My hand weakly reaches to her frame but falls as I scratch at the dirt.

Oliver's face turns away from me as a harsh tone bites at her words. "Trying doesn't matter if there are no results."

Growl after growl erupts in my stomach as I bash my head into the dust. *She's right. She's so damn right and I can't do anything about it.*

"So, you came to retrieve me," I groan as my paws shake against my chest, "because you're the Butcher's mutt."

"You can say that," Oliver says, gesturing to the gloomy boy who came along with her. "But I also came across quite the surprise when I met him. You two aren't very alike."

The boy towers over me with dark, brown eyes fuelling with fury as his stare drills into me. Wild, savage, black strands drape his face as his bruised, and muddied, sand skin fills my vision.

My fangs glimmer in the room's blinding lights as a hoarse snarl escapes my lips. "I don't know who-"

"Are five years so long, you've forgotten your own brother's face?" The boy snaps, digging his fingers into his ripped clothing to avoid his claws from attacking my face. Thick, bushy brows darken his amber eyes brewing with fury, as long, dark eyelashes bat roughly against his skin.

A thin, triangular face, with faint brown freckles dotting his cheeks; his beak nose, large temple, and pale, pink lips. If it weren't for the dirt and deep-embedded eyebags overlaying his skin, he would've been considered handsome.

My heart sinks as balls of saliva thicken in my throat. "Daniel?"

The boy's glare digs deeper, crawling under my skin, as if my words added to his rage, and he sarcastically spits, "Who else could I be?"

I don't want to believe it; I want to be wrong. My fingers quiver as I'm eager to erase his frame from my vision. Under his gaze, the desperation to sink into the floor and disappear is great. Drugged, weak, and pathetic. The brother he'd once idolised is now the opposite of what I've become. One broken and useless toy out of many others. The result of what this place does to you – using you until you can't stand anymore with batteries refusing to function, until your decisions begin to malfunction, until they batter the controller to micro-sized pieces.

So, why?

The replacement doll added to their collection.

The new-furnished toy with running batteries and a functioning controller.

'The human's entertainment.'

Why does it have to be you, Daniel?

THE BROKEN HOUND

is voice is unrecognisable. His sharp tone, his cold face, the way he looks at me, a swirling storm of anger and hatred, it's foreign. My paws slide along the grey walls and extend my blood lines, as we walk further in a seeming less never-ending tunnel. Mutters from Beast Tamers sound behind the walls, as well as the occasional guttural cries from werewolves, reaches our ears. *We must be behind the Butchers' Quarters.* My body shudders and shrinks with every step as I

follow obediently behind Oliver's black silhouette. She paces with long strides, distancing herself metres apart from me as if portraying the limits of my 'usefulness' and 'pride.' My head cranes to Daniel, matching my snail's pace. His tangled, wavy tresses dress over his face, as eerily as a ghost, as he drags his feet across the stone floor.

"How old are you?" I ask, eyeing his maroon eyes glowering at me with every breath I took.

"What do you think?" he retorts, shaking the hair out of his face.

Fifteen. But I don't want to believe it. Why did you accept the foundation's letter? Living a peaceful, quiet life in the community would've been better, so why do you have to come here out of all places? Though, as I take in his skinny figure towering over me with a face full of resentment, I realise I'm the stupid one. It's been so long, and I hadn't realised. I face his furious dark pupils, and a soft whimper leaves my throat.

"Daniel…" I begin – *if you are him.* "I don't know if you've realised, but this place is a slaughterhouse."

"I can see that," Daniel says icily, breaking his eye contact with me.

"Then-"

"But I'm not going." he finalizes.

I stare questionably at the giant draped in tattered clothing. He overlooks my four-legged body as my face twists and brows heighten.

"I'm doing this to protect you!" I bark as my muzzle scrunches with white fangs baring at his bony figure.

Daniel scans my frame with a sheer look of disgust, making my growl lower.

"Is that what you told yourself all these years?" he asks, an iciness latching onto the tip of his words. "Looks like it worked well."

"I couldn't get out." I pull myself back as he steps forward.

"You chose not to."

Needles arise from my mane as my hind leg hits against the wall.

"Of course, who would go back to a community living in the slums when luxury's right in front of you?" Daniel scoffs, weighing his knee into my shoulder.

My head lowers as my ears flatten against my coat. *Luxury? This?* A sick growl rumbles in my stomach, and I lock eyes with Daniel.

"It's been long. I know, and I'm sorry." I stiffly state as Daniel's knee digs deeper into my collar.

"So, you admit it?" Daniel asks with a soft smile dressing his face and flashing eyes rumbling as if containing a hurricane.

My throat tightens as his knee bone pushes against my throat. *You're not even giving me a chance to speak.*

"I just want you to get out of here," I choke.

"Why should I?"

"You're my brother-"

"We're not even related by blood," Daniel interjects, listening to my painful gasps as he lifts his knee and catches up to Oliver who's in disappearing distance.

My heart clenches. So, the time we spent as a pack, the promise we made through Pack Code, everything I did for you, are you telling me it was all useless!? My paws clatter against the pavement as I scamper towards Daniel.

"Why!?" I yell as a hoarse cough follows after. "Why are you like this!? Everything I did was for you!"

"Gabriel, would you like the other werewolves to find you!?" Oliver hisses with a scowl across her face.

"Let them!" I snap, my fangs glistening in the darkness. *This fool needs a lesson first.*

"For me?" Daniel asks, his brown eyes converting to a deadly crimson hue, "Had it ever occurred to you, that instead, you might be hurting me!?"

Daniel's jaw cracks as fangs the size of kitchen knives prop from his mouth. "That instead, the many times you left me, put me in danger of being killed!?" Spikes protrude from his body as his tail thrashes against the stone floor.

"What are you, 5!?" I snarl, the adrenaline rushing through my veins, "You're old enough to look after yourself!"

Veins pop at the back of Daniel's hands as his claws dig into my tufts of fur. My claws extend to his deformed face, and before I reach him, he slams me into the hard stone.

"I'm an Omega!" he screams, my blood dripping from his extended nails, "Can you still say the same?"

High beeps of a lorry sound beside us as its blinding lights flash against my eyes. The engine revs, backing into the garage as if muting the pounding of my heart, clobbering against my ribcage. With the incapability of dampening my throat, my mouth lies agape as Daniel's eyes of fury stab my soul. I lift my body from the ground and shake my coat; *I'm thankful to Oliver for bringing us here.*

"Grow up, quit acting like a spoiled brat," I growl. "An Omega doesn't need others to survive.

Don't tarnish the reputation of every Omega, just because you can't do anything on your own!"

Cardboard boxes clatter as my body hits against them, splattering fresh, fruit products onto my mane. Pain slithers up my spine as whines escape from my muzzle, and I scrabble against the floor once Daniel dashes towards me with bared fangs.

"You're not even an Omega, don't act as if you understand!" he snarls, flinging my body into the wall like a flimsy ragdoll.

Black pours into my vision, and the world blurs. My body trembles from the impact as I struggle to keep my eyes open. *Open them, open your eyes!* The earth's distortion gradually comes to a stop as I lift myself off the ground, and a huff escapes my torn nostrils.

"I waited five years! Of bullying, of being shunned, no matter what I did, every werewolf was stronger than me, and that's the first thing, *you* out of *all* people, have to say!?"

The earth quivers as Daniel sprints on all-fours towards my body. A box knocks against his head as I dart to the white ropes hanging at the corner of the garage. Daniel's growl deepens as he shakes off the stings from his orange mane, and he chases after me.

"To be a target, to never feel safe." Glowering red eyes pierce through me as Daniel pursues me, "To be in pain, to be weak, to worry about your death, each and every damn day, how the hell would you know how that feels!?"

My back leg shivers as Daniel's fangs pierce into it. Stings escalate my body, and I clamp my teeth into his muzzle as he loosens his grip.

"I wouldn't be helping you escape if I didn't!" I scream, floundering in his grasp.

I have regrets about Kanya every day, every minute, every second I close my eyes! Daniel's paws swipe at me as thick, white ropes entangle his body.

"I just want you to get out of here, alive, Daniel! Why's that so hard to ask?" My legs are eager to buckle. I'm using all my body weight to pull Daniel's body to the lorry. Scarlet decorates the white fabric as they cut my black gums and trim my teeth. The world turns as I totter to the truck's wheel and tie the rope around the tires.

Daniel flounders in the material and curses. "You can't tell me what to do-"

His figure is no more than a black line now. Coughs erupt from my chest, as my system burns with flames scorching my lungs and my heart swelters from the burning heat. My throat is tight and dehydrated like dry sand, despite the metallic taste of blood overlaying my tongue.

"At least do it for me…" I beg, with a wolfish grin working its way on my face. The leather necklace lifts from my chest as I throw it over Daniel's head. The wolf tooth, wrapped in leather, buries itself in Daniel's orange fur as he looks at me with a horror-stricken face. I place a paw onto Daniel's one with blood cascading from my nose, and raspy pants escape my lips. "Please."

THE LONE WOLF'S LAST CRY

o!" Daniel thrashes against the lorry, fighting against the ropes binding him, as screams erupt from his throat.

My tongue lolls onto the chilled ground as sweat pours down my body. "Daniel..." The cold wind brushes against my coat as darkness clouds my vision. Like a bomb detonating, my body burns as if adding oil to a fire. "I'm sorry."

"I don't want your apology!" Daniel yells, tightening the rope wounding his body faster than before.

My paws twitch from the continuous seizures shattering my system as a hammering pain splits my brain. *I can't move.* Tears line my eyelids as slaughterous stings eat me alive, and my ears ring, making me eager to sleep, to enter an eternal slumber, but Daniel is still there. *I can't- not yet.*

"How many times do you have to leave me to be satisfied!?" he shouts, adding to the pains puncturing my brain.

A dry cough escalates my throat as blood smears my tongue, and ragged pants escape my lips. "If it's for you," I croak, forcing the rise and descend of my chest, "as many times as I have to." A small gleam twinkles in my eyes as a smug grin lines my face. "I'm hopeless, aren't I?" I say, choking on the endless amounts of blood bubbling in my chest. "Without you, do you think I'd survive this hell alone?"

"Stop!" Daniel screams. "Stop! Curse me, hate me! I just found you! I can't-"

Daniel's voice is faint, dispersing into the air as soft as a whisper as blood erupts from my guts and clogs my throat. My head is the weight of a feather, and my body, a burning furnace. Part of it is going numb.

"I can't be alone!" Daniel cries, his voice cracking from the tearing of his throat, "Not again, I can't-"

I left you for five years. Denied visiting you because I was too eager to please you. Used you as an excuse for my selfish reasons, and now look at me. I can't even thank you for finding me.

"Daniel," I wheeze, moving my head towards the frustrated grunts of my younger brother. "Omegas are weak."

My eyes close as I attempt to swallow the blood brewing in my throat. If Kanya was alive, and I acted differently- if I didn't let her go that night, would she tell Daniel, a werewolf like her, something different?

"You think I don't know!? Being an Omega is nothing better than dirt!" Daniel shouts, "We're whores!"

I know.

"Food supply!"

I know.

"Training equipment!"

I know.

"Don't talk as if you understand how that feels!"

A tear dribbles down my mane as I gasp.

"I know," I croak, every mouth movement breaking my body, "but Daniel, I want you to live. No matter how hard it is, survive, idiot."

The lorry engine revs as the tires squeal against the pavement, and Daniel's thrashing is heavier than before.

"You can't just- what about Pack Code!? I thought you had pride as a wolf!"

My body slumps as Oliver hauls me over her shoulder and carries me to her department. The lorry rumbles, driving out of the garage, and I'm hoping it takes Daniel to the actual place our ancestors call 'home'.

"Gabi!" Daniel screams, and my aching heart tears, as salty droplets drip down my muzzle.

I'm sorry. Daniel's yells are only slight, and my body shakes in Oliver's hold as the cold breeze caresses my fur. My tired eyes train on the cloak of darkness fuelled with Daniel's muffled screams, and a whine bubbles in my throat.

My brother.

My pack.

My lifeline.

From the foundation's admissions to bringing you to The Outside World – don't think I regret a single thing I've done for you; *I don't.* Yet, I'm a useless brother, making you trust in me all these years for nothing, nothing except vain anticipation. *I'm sorry.*

Daniel's voice dissipates in the booming of the garage's shutters closing as a soft whimper leaves my lips. But out of all the things I've done, The Outside World – the legend of our ancestors, the beauty of the 'real word' we spent long nights fantasising about, the paradise we could only find in torn, used books - it might be selfish of me to think now, but… really…*I wish I could've seen it with you, too… Daniel.*

The werewolves' journey continues in…

THE BLOODHOUND'S SERVANT

MORE INFORMATION ON THE
BLOODHOUND'S SERVANT

Weak is a word that describes you. It doesn't define who you are.

With the last name of his brother being the only confirmation of their bond, Daniel Louvell is forced to enter the hell he fears most; a new pack. With new rules and guidelines, and a leader to follow, Daniel takes the risk of working his way up the ranks as the lowest of all werewolves, the Omega. Though, with hard work comes great sacrifice, and in a family of famished werewolves, hungering for power, it won't be easy to become the top without being ravished by their greed. Status is everything, and in order to fight - the 'puny, pushover, and weakling Omega, Daniel Louvell,' will have to exist no more.

THE BLOODHOUND'S DUOLOGY

ABOUT THE AUTHOR

Grace Okot, also known as 'GALADIN' on social media, is an aspiring dark fantasy author who has been writing fictional short stories from a young age. Her work, The Reaper's Bloodhound, first novel of The Bloodhound's Duology had been submitted to many writing competitions including the Bridport Prize Competition. She has a love for fantastical creatures and myths, and loves nothing more than reading with a hot cup of milk as she delves into the world of fiction.

 Instagram | gala._.din

 Youtube | GALADIN

Printed in Great Britain
by Amazon

77120780R00113